The Insatiable Man

THE INSATIABLE MAN

A Novella

Adam Philip Stern

iUniverse, Inc.
New York Lincoln Shanghai

The Insatiable Man
A Novella

Copyright © 2007 by Adam Philip Stern

All rights reserved. No part of this book may be used or reproduced by any means, graphic, electronic, or mechanical, including photocopying, recording, taping or by any information storage retrieval system without the written permission of the publisher except in the case of brief quotations embodied in critical articles and reviews.

iUniverse books may be ordered through booksellers or by contacting:

iUniverse
2021 Pine Lake Road, Suite 100
Lincoln, NE 68512
www.iuniverse.com
1-800-Authors (1-800-288-4677)

This is a work of fiction. All of the characters, names, incidents, organizations, and dialogue in this novel are either the products of the author's imagination or are used fictitiously.

ISBN-13: 978-0-595-43219-6 (pbk)
ISBN-13: 978-0-595-87560-3 (ebk)
ISBN-10: 0-595-43219-0 (pbk)
ISBN-10: 0-595-87560-2 (ebk)

Printed in the United States of America

To my parents for supporting me in everything I do,
and to my brother for consistently setting the bar so high

I have a plan. In my head, it goes like this: I come upon a time machine—I'm not sure how, but that's not important right now. I figure out the exact moment when some guy said to his lady friend, "you know what might be interesting? Monogamy. I'd like to try that for a while." And I go back thousands of years to that precise time and location, say hello to the man, and proceed to bludgeon him to death with a large stone or boulder of some sort.

This man has clearly ruined my life. The way I see it, until that point, men took as many lovers as they could handle, and it was all perfectly legit. Women understood; that was just The Deal. After all, men have an evolutionarily predisposed *need* to spread their seed. Maybe the women even joked about The Deal at the beauty parlor, if such a thing existed. You know, "Oh, that Marvin! He'd have trouble pleasing three women, let alone the whole dozen!" And when I said that they took as many women as they could "handle," I didn't mean handle like abuse or boss around or anything. I meant provide for, care for, be a loving and good father for their children sort of handle. It all seems like a perfect system governed by human nature. The men whom were successful, either because they were strong and athletic and could hunt well, or because they were cunning businessmen or whatever, would obviously be more attractive and would get more women than their geeky, nerdy, socially impaired counterparts, and so it would go. The human race would evolve properly and everyone would be happy.

But then this stupid, desperate son of a bitch—he was probably one of the most repulsive around—came around and had to muck everything up. He thought, "gee, I'll never get women cause I'm a loser, and I have no muscle tone. I need a gimmick." And he found it by offering something no other man on the planet would ever concede: commitment.

The conversation probably went like this:

"Hey there, pretty lady."

The pretty lady stares incredulously at the puny man standing in front of her shocked that he would even try to talk to her.

"What do you want?"

"I want you to be my wife."

"Why on earth would I be *your* wife?"

"Because I promise that you will be the only woman I will ever sleep with for the rest of my life if you choose to be with me."

The woman was stunned. Even with his repugnance staring her in the face, this was an offer that was too good to resist. One man, whom *she* could boss around and manipulate to her heart's delight. She recalled her current situation, where she shared the attention, wealth, and love of a good looking man with seven other women. She decided she would accept the offer.

It was at that moment that true marital happiness died for the rest of eternity. It probably wasn't long before the woman told all of her girl friends about how great it was having a man all to herself, and pretty soon they all demanded the same thing. Before you knew it, the entire female population was decrying "monogamy or bust!" And that is why I will never be happy.

See, I can't stand commitment. Don't get me wrong; I expect complete fidelity on *her* end. But for men, it just doesn't seem fair. We're programmed to constantly want new women, like little boys are programmed to wrestle with each other. It's all part of God's master plan and this schmuck who wasn't getting lucky some umpteen thousand years ago screwed it up for everyone. Now I'm stuck with a residual evolutionary fear of monogamy in a society that not only condones it, but makes a mockery of men who are only fulfilling their evolutionary duty.

Now, you women out there, go ahead; roll your eyes and shake your head with disapproval. Curse my immaturity, and laugh at the silliness of my views—I don't mind. It doesn't bother me because I know that your male counterparts are nodding along, furtively agreeing with me. Ask them how they feel about my stance and they'll deny it, but they and I both know the truth. Ladies, I've heard your arguments, and to be honest, I'm not all that persuaded by them. But we'll get to that later.

Right now, I'm in an especially dangerous rut because I'm seeing a girl, Maya, whom my head tells me could be *the* one. She's attractive, engaging, intelligent, faithful, and most important of all, we can talk for hours without a dull moment or awkward silence. I know that she's terrific, and let's be honest, I may be overachieving a bit—yet still, there is something, some force, always lying beneath the surface, which won't allow me to be happy in a long term relationship no matter how good I know it is.

Is this how all twenty one year olds at college think?

"No. You're a fuckin' nut case."

Silverstein. Completely shallow, ridiculously crude, and the source of my comic relief during my three years at school.

"So you never feel suffocated then?"

"What like this?"

Silverstein grabs a pillow and leaps on top of me, smothering me. As I struggle to get him off me and gasp for air, I realize what a silly question I had posed. Of course, Silverstein never feels suffocated; he's never been on a second date. He's never been on a first date, for that matter. The only times Silverstein gets lucky is when there is lots of alcohol, dark lighting, and desperation involved.

Finally I hurl him off of me and onto the tiled floor below.

"Get off me you tubby bastard."

"Hey!" He feigns being offended. "What did I say?"

"You're just carrying around some holiday weight, I know."

It's October. Does Columbus Day weekend involve eating more than usual? I don't think so.

Silverstein notices a freshman in just a towel walking down the hall toward the communal bathroom. His eyes widen, and he springs to his feet. I already know what he's going to do. He flashes me a sinister look and a cockeyed grin. After a momentary pause, he follows the kid into the bathroom and two minutes later returns to our room with the freshman's towel in hand. He waves it in front of me triumphantly.

"How many is that?"

"Twelve this week. Damn these frosh are unsuspecting."

It's Silverstein's fault that we're stuck in this stupid freshman dorm as seniors. He was supposed to submit the paperwork for our off-campus housing to reslife by a certain deadline and he didn't, and of course by that time the housing lottery had already taken place and bam! Here I am, surrounded by freshmen and the Towel Assassin, as he likes to be known. Personally, I think Silverstein has way too much fun under these less than desirable circumstances.

I stand up and put my shoes on.

"Where you going?"

"Gotta meet Maya at the Snack Hut."

"But, Matt, you're gonna miss the naked freshfucker run down the—"

"It's okay, I've seen it eleven times before."

Silverstein appears legitimately disappointed that I don't share his interest in watching a horrified and embarrassed freshman sprint down the hall naked trying to make it back to his room unseen.

I put on my coat and exit the room. I'm already dreading having to spend the next hour and a half with Maya, for no reason whatsoever.

"Matty!"

I turn to see what he wants.

"Yeah?"

"Squeeze her ass for me, eh?"

"Sure thing, bud."

Silverstein's face erupts in hysterics and I immediately know the circumstances which I am about to face. As I turn around, the naked freshman, clutching his privates, sprints awkwardly past me toward his room.

"Must be cold out there!"

It's ridiculous how proud Silverstein is of himself, but I can't help but smile.

When I arrive at the Snack Hut, I see Maya perusing the food bar with Gilbert. Ugh, Gilbert. What a tool. They don't notice me as I sneak up behind them, so I pinch Maya's right butt cheek and she yelps.

"That was from Silverstein."

Her shock turns to approving rebellion as she grabs my hips and kisses me.

"Get a room!"

Shut up, Gilbert.

"Oh, hey, Gil."

"Do you have any credit?" Asks Maya.

She's starving but has no meal plan credit left on her card so I give her mine so she can have some snacks. Then we make our way to a table and sit down.

"So, you should stay over tonight," she states rather matter-of-factly.

Maya's got an off-campus place that she shares with Gilbert and two girls, Molly and Lauren.

I shoot her a quizzical look. Why am I fighting this?

"I've got an exam on Thursday and I've got the night shift Friday, so I've got to get my Matt time in."

Suddenly I love this girl. She may as well have just said that we've got to get our sex out of the way tonight so she can ace her Orgo exam (which way down the road will allow her physician's salary to support me monetarily) and spend her weekend night volunteering to help people at EMS. How could I even think about abandoning this girl?

"Sounds good to me."

"I'm seeing Victor tonight."

Nobody cares!

"That's cool, man. What you doing?" Hating a gay person doesn't make me homophobic, right? There are lots of gay people who are fine—better than fine. Great, grand, wonderful. Gilbert's just not one of them. Maya always told me that every girl should have a gay best friend. And I think that's great, but Gilbert's indisputably annoying completely regardless of his sexual orientation.

Gilbert's been babbling for what seems like at least half an hour when I notice That Girl. She's the one who's always lying out in a bikini on the green if it's sunny (temperature doesn't really seem to affect her) or on the elliptical trainer at the gym wearing nothing but a sports bra when it's nasty out. God, what I would give to—

Wait. Wait. Wait. Maya. My girlfriend. Damn it.

That Girl picks up some yogurt and starts to flirt with a bunch of muscle heads perhaps only enrolled at this school so the wealthy alumni can brag to each other about how well the basketball team is doing this year. I look back at Maya, and she seems utterly plain.

***

Maya's Matt time met expectations. By that I mean that it was good, as coitus and canoodling tends to be—though it wasn't particularly ground-breaking, earth shattering, or revolutionary. Much like the revolution and to Silverstein's dismay, it was not televised, but I digress. When I'm with Maya, I'm legitimately attracted to her and I feel that our time together is generally enjoyable for both parties. Something happens to this feeling thirty seconds after the sex is over. It's the same process that *always* occurs in situations like this: I begin to feel suffocated. She hugs me tight and rests her head on my chest, and as I stroke her hair gently, all I can think of is how much I'd like to get back to my room, have some beers with Silverstein, play the latest football game on the latest video game system, and go to sleep (alone, in my own spacious and comfortable bed).

What conflicts me now, is that not only do I want to leave the room, but the relationship as well. That Girl just seems so appealing, so full of mystery, and exotic intrigue—and I'm not saying that I could get That Girl because I'm pretty sure I couldn't, unless it were under Silverstein circumstances. But I am pretty sure that I'd enjoy the single life. I think that I'm ready to hit the market again, go out on Friday nights not knowing whom I might go home with—it all seems so exciting compared to sex by appointment, which remains responsible, but slightly less stimulating than the DMV's driving safety course.

It's about when I start picturing what life would be like socializing like Silverstein that my mind finally kicks in and does something useful. I remember how empty random hook ups can be, and I remember how awful droughts are. I remind myself that being with Maya means guaranteed action! Why would I want to give up a guarantee? And then it happens.

"What are you thinking?" She asks.

Oh, God. Please kill me. Please.

"Nothing really."

"No, really. What were you thinking?"

"Just how lucky I am to have you."

Nice save, Matty boy. Nice save, indeed.

***

Parents weekend was last weekend. Were my parents here? No. And do you know why? Because they always come a week late. They do this because they enjoy taking my friends out, and they couldn't do that while they were all out with their own parents, which is pretty nice of them when you think about it. I guess.

So, my dad has me make a reservation at the Asian Nirvana for eight: Me, Mom, Dad, Richard (my older brother), Seth (my younger brother), Maya, Silverstein, and D.A. D.A. is Silverstein and my closest friend I'd say. We call him that because he's a dumb ass, though he thinks it's because he asks a lot of questions and wants to be a district attorney some day. I admit, sometimes we're not the most mature kids at our institution.

Meanwhile, these dinners are always stressful for me because I have so many fronts to be worried about. It starts relatively benignly. I pick on Seth a little bit, and Richard rolls his eyes a lot. Mom's pretty quiet as she's studying the wine list (which I'm pretty sure is written entirely in Vietnamese), and Maya, Silverstein, and D.A. are all getting along fine.

Then the questions start from Dad.

"So which one of you is, eh, Mr. Silverstein?"

"Jesus, Pop. You've met him like four hundred times. He was my freshman roommate for Christ's sake."

"Yeah, but look at the two of them," he replies as he gestures toward Silverstein and D.A. "They're practically twins."

For the record, they look nothing alike. Silverstein is short and fat with a dirty blonde crew cut, and D.A. looks like Ralph Macchio.

As a matter of fact, I tried to switch his nickname to Ralph, but it got shot down.

"I'm Mr. Silverstein," points out the non-Karate Kid looking one rather condescendingly.

"So you must be the district attorney?" Asks my father in D.A.'s direction.

"You bet." He's proud.

Dad's done with the boys. He's much more excited to focus on Maya, whom he figures I'm destined to marry.

"And Miss Maya, looking lovely I see."

She doesn't seem embarrassed, but she must be. Regardless, I'm embarrassed for her.

"Thank you, Mr. Quibley."

"Maya," he stares at her with a disapproving look. "How long have you been seeing Matt?"

"About a year and a half."

"And how long have you known me?"

"About a year, I guess."

"And you still can't bring yourself to call me, Bob?"

"Sorry, Mister—" she catches herself. "Bob."

He smiles and is truly content with himself.

"So have you kids given any thought to your future?"

Notice he uses the singular "future." Obviously one future, not two.

"Matt wants to be an astronaut!" Silverstein chimes in. He thinks it's funny that I interned for NASA and have aspirations to work there some day. I hush him up.

"How do you mean, Dad?"

I know exactly how he means.

"Well you know, Maya, our eldest son Richard married his college girlfriend."

"I'm sitting right here, Dad." Richard is quiet, and it's easy to forget that he's around, but it doesn't mean he appreciates it.

"I'll give you five thousand dollars."

"Jesus, Bob!" Even my tipsy mother is outraged at Dad's inappropriateness.

"For a honeymoon! You think the plane tickets and the hotels in Hawaii are going to pay for themselves?"

Mom still can't believe what has transpired. For once, I'm with her. She buries her head in her hands.

"Well, they're not!"

My father's train of thought has got me thinking. They say that forty's the new thirty, and thirty's the new twenty. Well, twenty's got to be the new something. So if we're going to draw a linear relationship here, twenty's the new ten, so why am I thinking about marriage? Oh, right. I'm not. He is. Dad is implying that we should return to the days when kids got married at puberty, and I guess that would be fine except for the fact that most of them died in their thirties. I'm not so cool with that aspect of the plan.

The dinner continues along in a similar manner for about an hour. Mom gets inebriated. Dad pressures Maya and me to get married as soon as we graduate while we try to fend him off as politely as we can. Silverstein and D.A. are both utterly bored, but truly appreciate a free meal. This is especially true of Silverstein whose latest attempt at a diet is on hiatus because "the Sabbath obviously doesn't count." Is Asian Nirvana what the Bible had in mind for a Shabbat dinner?

I'm horrified by the whole event, but my peers seem to ignore the fact that anything weird transpired at all. By the end of the dinner, I escort Maya to EMS head quarters and my parents head to the hotel. They allow fifteen year old Seth to stay with me for the night, which is something he's been looking forward to since last year when Silverstein got him drunk and made him hook up with a fat chick at a party.

It's the night of AnarFling, a themed party given by our school's chapter of the Anarchists of America (For the record, I think it's a little hypocritical for anarchists to have an association.), and it's widely known as one of the wildest times all semester. People show up half naked. Others wear absurd combinations of inappropriate clothes like a sports coat and tie with no shirt, or a normal top with nothing but tighty whities below. Everyone's quite liquored up at this annual event, and to be honest, you have to be if you're going to have a good time. To sum up, it's Silverstein's favorite night of the year.

Anyway, what kind of big brother would I be if I didn't take Seth to an event like this? Needless to say, we picked up a handle of rum and a bottle of coke on the way back to the dorm and began pre-gaming. My brother is a light weight, so he began slurring his words after the second drink. But he was determined to keep up with Silverstein, D.A., and me—so after a few, drinks, he was beginning to look like a proper drunk. Poor kid. I shouldn't judge; before long I was a proper drunk, too.

The night was a blur. I remember dancing in a corner all by myself. I can recall seeing Seth sneak a swig of some girl's flask and thinking that maybe this wasn't the best idea but at the same time being pretty proud of him. I definitely remember seeing my AM184 TA dancing in the middle of the room. She looked hot, sporting what can only be described as lingerie. I think I danced with her, but I'm not sure if the memory of that is from before or after I passed out so it may have been a dream. That Girl made an appearance, too—or at least, someone who vaguely resembled her. There's a poor man's That Girl on campus somewhere whom I sometimes mistake for That Girl if I'm looking at her from a distance, as I often am. Nevertheless, the right breast of either That Girl or her protégé Poor Man's That Girl was seen flopping around in all its glory. Normally I would assume this was a dream, but I still remember it pretty clearly so I'm going to go and put it among my top ten favorite moments of life (real life, that is, not dream life). The last thing I do remember is a vague image of Maya in her EMS uniform. It doesn't all make sense right away, but I have an alarming fear that it will all add up soon—and not in a good way.

***

My head is throbbing when I awake at 8:27AM. Damn you alcohol. Where am I? What happened last night? I have this feeling that I should remember something, that something did *happen*, but the exact memory is just out of reach.

A quick assessment reveals that I'm in my own bed, and this comforts me. I look around the room to find Silverstein looking at porn on his computer. No sign of Seth.

"Where's Seth?"

He doesn't turn around to look at me.

"Look at the rack on this—"

"Hey. Look at me."

"It says it's that girl we saw on TV in that music video, but I don't think I believe it."

"It's not her."

"It says it right here."

"Why would she pose naked for your skeevy porn site?"

"Maybe they blackmailed her about something."

I've had enough.

"Silverstein!"

Now I've got his attention. He turns around and leaps toward me like an excited little kid. His face is one of pure exhilaration. He can't wait to tell me about the night we just had.

"Dude!"

"Where's Seth?"

"Health services."

Shit.

"Why? What happened?"

"Drank too much. Puked on Minnie Simmons," he says with a smile and a snicker.

"They didn't take him to the hospital?"

"Nah, your girl came and cleaned him up, made him sleep it off in a university bed."

"Maya *was* there. Yes. Okay."

"You better hope she didn't see you."

"Why?"

Another sinister smile on his end. I loathe this.

"You really don't remember?"

"I remember some things."

I remember nothing.

"You and that calc TA."

"Go on."

"Well, allow me do a reenactment."

Using his hands as puppets, Silverstein proceeds to recreate the event.

"'Hey, Matt. You're so good at math.' 'Hi, calc TA. You ain't so bad yourself.' 'Wanna make out?' 'Okay!'"

And for at least thirty seconds while I try to get a grip on the situation his hands make out with each other.

"I made out with the girl who grades my calc assignments?"

"It was disgusting."

"Did Maya see?"

"How should I know? I had my own problems last night."

"What problems?"

Silverstein launches into his post adventure recollection routine. This may be even more enjoyable for him than the actual event.

"So there I am, minding my own business at AnarFling." I specifically remember seeing Silverstein accosting and harassing innocent freshman girls, but I let it slide. "When this girl comes right up to me and starts grinding to some nineties rock—definitely not grinding music. But I say, 'what the hey,' and I go with it. Nice body on this girl, can't really see her face. We grind for a while, and I whisper into her ear, 'Wanna get out of here,' ya know? And she doesn't respond. So I figure, okay, she doesn't want to leave yet, maybe she's not that into me."

"You? How could that be?"

"You shush now. So we dance some more, and again, I say, 'wanna head out?' louder this time. Again, nothing. No, 'fuck off.' No, 'not right now, maybe later.' Just more dancing. I'm not sure what to make of it so I just keep going with it. Before I know it, they're kicking everyone out of the party, and the lights are on. So first I notice that whatever semblance of clothing this girl was wearing on top is gone, and second, I see that her *entire* face is covered in acne."

Arrrghhh.

"Not just regular acne, but like meta-acne, ya know? Like pimples on top of pimples and stuff. But I'm drunk, so who cares, right?"

I just shake my head.

"Well anyway, I take my tie off and cover her up as best I can with it."

"Why didn't you just give her your jacket?"

"Shit, man. It was cold out last night."

"Fair enough."

"So we get outside, and she says, in a deep a throaty voice, 'HAVE YOU SEEN MY FRIENDS?'"

He does the imitation, and already I know what's coming. Something is off about this voice, and it usually means one thing.

"And that's when I realize, this girl is deaf!"

Silverstein gets excited by anything that's a little absurd. He'd never hooked up with a deaf girl, and this was his chance.

"Now, I have no idea where her friends are. So I look her straight on and mouth, 'let's go back to your place.' And we do. And as we're walking toward her apartment, I suddenly get this tremendous wave of guilt, like hooking up with an ugly girl just because she's deaf might not be the most honorable thing, ya know?"

"Yeah, I guess, I can see what you mean."

You sick bastard.

"But I'm determined to go through with it. So she leads me into her room, and we start making out."

He looks around the room as if to make sure no one else is around.

"Now at this point," he continues, "I'm not even really that drunk anymore, and I'm definitely starting to doubt the whole plan—considering the meta-acne and everything."

"Right."

"But she's not the worst kisser, so I stick around for a bit. For a moment, I even forget that she's deaf, which is why I was there in the first place. And then it happens."

I roll my eyes in anticipation.

"In that same, deep, throaty, voice, she says, 'PLEASURE ME!' And that's it for me. At this point, I freak out. I've got to get outta there, ya know? So I jump off the sofa causing her to lose her balance and fall off, down onto the floor."

"Jesus, Silverstein!"

"It gets worse."

How? How can it possibly get worse?

"While she's getting her bearings after the fall, I pick up my jacket, tie, and—"

"Wait. Wasn't the tie wrapped around her?"

"Yeah, I pulled it off of her and stuffed it into my pocket. And then, she says, 'WHERE ARE YOU GOING?' and I mouth something back about having to wake up for church tomorrow, and I jet the heck out of there."

"You're going to church? On a Saturday?"

"Yeah, well, I better—I'm pretty sure I've sinned."

I grin back at him and put a hand on his shoulder. That's the thing about Silverstein; he may be a real ass, but he makes me laugh—and if laughter's the best medicine as they say, I'm happy to be a Silverstein pill popper.

***

I go to health services to check on my brother. The nurse on duty allows me to see him. When I enter the room, I notice he's awake already. He is slumped over the side of the bed with his face buried in his hands.

"Rough night, little brother?"

He can't even turn to me.

"You have no idea."

"I've been there, believe me."

I refresh his cup of water and hand it to him.

"Drink up, Seth. We're meeting Mom and Dad for breakfast in an hour."

Just then, I see Maya in the corridor. She looks exhausted, trudging down the hallway in her EMS uniform. Did she notice me and walk by anyway without saying a word? Does she know about my alleged indiscretions? I have to find out.

I stand up and jog after her.

"Maya!"

She turns and looks at me as if I'm just one more obstacle on the way to her impending collapse.

"Wait up."

I try to read her face but it's completely covered by a fatigued facade. No emotion, no anger, just exhaustion.

"Rough night?"

She nods.

"I heard you took care of Seth last night. Thanks."

"What else would an EMT do on her Friday night shift at an Ivy League school?"

"How many calls did you get?"

She recalls the various "emergencies."

"Five. Four drunks and a kid who sliced his arm hopping the front gates."

"Didn't get any sleep then?"

She shakes her head. I'm not getting any rage coming from her, but maybe she's just too tired. I wonder if I should tell her about Tangent X or if that would just be pointless (I've decided to refer to my calculus TA as Tangent X because a. it's a relevant code name, b. it makes her sound like a comic book character, and c. because she represents the first tangential line of infidelity that I've ever committed in my life. Granted, explanation c. is a bit of a stretch.).

"Hey, listen." I put an arm around her waist to see if there's any resistance (no more than usual), and continue, "go home, get some sleep. Can we meet up for lunch at about three?"

"Sure. Tell Seth to take it easy 'til his tolerance is better than that of a five year old girl."

With that advice, she turns and walks away. No hug, no kiss. Mystery remains unsolved.

After breakfast and farewells are finished with the family, I run into Molly, one of the girls Maya lives with. I like her; she always gives me a big hello. Today, though, she's on her way to the gym and can't talk, but seems terribly frustrated with me.

"Wait!" I scream as she begins to jog off to the gym. "Why the cold shoulder, Molly?"

"You know why."

She saw me with Tangent X.

"Oh, that. Yeah."

"Maybe I'm missing part of the story here, Matt, but frankly, you disgust me."

I never liked that Molly very much.

"Molly," I plead.

"No. You do. I can't even stand the sight of you. Have you told her yet?"

"You think I need to?"

She becomes outraged and slaps me with both hands across the chest.

"I was kidding!"

I wasn't kidding.

"I haven't seen her yet, but I'll tell her as soon as I can find her."

It was a gray lie. Whereas a white lie spares someone else's feelings, a gray lie makes you feel less bad about your own.

I spent the next few hours imagining all of the possible scenarios which could follow from an admission of guilt. There was the chance that she'd stab me with the butter knife which lay in front of her, though I never pinned Maya as the violent type. Another possibility was the hysterical crying reaction. What is with girls and crying? They cry about silly, stupid things, and sometimes they cry over nothing at all, literally. I hate it when girls cry about anything in my presence, let alone a legitimate cry as a result of my indiscretions. Then I thought, maybe she'll break up with me as soon as I tell her.

This option seemed almost appealing. This way, I wouldn't have to feel so guilty about constantly feeling suffocated anymore. I could live life on the prowl, preying on innocent college girls as I saw fit. Maybe I'd even see Tangent X again.

But to my surprise and slight disappointment, Maya didn't respond at all like I thought she would.

"I made out with a girl at AnarFling," I say as soon as we sit down at a table.

She stares back at me, without breaking eye contact even for a second, and thinks for a few seconds.

"Did it mean anything?"

"I don't understand."

"Um," she stalls as she searches for a language that will make sense to me. "I mean, do you like her?"

To be honest, I feel that the 'do you like her' question is even more bogus than the 'meaningful' question because the concept of 'liking' someone is really an invention of women. Men don't 'like' women. They just don't. They're attracted to women, and sometimes they even enjoy spending time with women, but I could feel this way about two hundred girls at school. Does that mean that I like two hundred girls? I bet that first guy—the one who was the first to offer commitment to only one woman—I bet he also told her that he 'liked' her, and that was the end of masculine superiority. From that moment on, women would have verbally manipulative powers that men simply were not smart enough to overcome. Sadly, again because of that fool thousands of years ago, I know the correct answer.

"No. I don't even know her. She's my calculus—"

"Stop. I don't want to know anything about her except that she doesn't mean anything to you."

"Right, okay."

"Okay, good. That's fine; I'm glad you told me."

Then she leans over the table and kisses me. What just happened, exactly? Why isn't she more outraged? Where is the fork in my forehead? Does she really just not care that much? Maybe she assumes that this is a common thing in college relationships; maybe cheating has become decriminalized in today's post-teenage world. Has she cheated? I don't think so, but now I wouldn't put it out of the realm of possibility.

The rest of our lunch is ordinary until we finish and I receive a text message on my cell.

FROM: *Tangent X*
> *hey u, had fun last nite, call me if you wanna get 2gether again*

Out of nowhere, I'm feeling more alive than I can remember feeling in months. I don't remember exchanging numbers with Tangent X last night, but I clearly did.

"You get a text?"

"Yep."

"Who from?"

"Just one of those promotional texts from the wireless company about accessing the internet over your phone or something."

Why am I lying? What am I hiding? I already told her that Tangent X means nothing to me.

Or does she? Maybe last night was the best night of my life and I just can't remember it because of the booze. Maybe I owe it to myself to see her again. Now that I think of it, Maya never asked me not to do it again. She explicitly said that all she wanted was to make sure that my fling with Tangent X didn't mean anything, and I've already explained that men are incapable of 'liking' women, so by my logic Maya has condoned my behavior as long as it doesn't evolve into a relationship that *means* something to me. As long as at any time, I'm willing to abandon it, it's legit and allowed.

But if there's nothing wrong with pursuing Tangent X, why am I feeling guilty about the rational decision I've just made?

***

Maya seemed determined to keep an eye on me Saturday night, which I guess is a pessimistic way to look at my girlfriend wanting to spend time with me after a rough Friday night with no 'Matt time.' Our common friends Dave and Robbie were throwing a traffic light party that night at their apartment, and I knew, despite my vociferous protests, that our attendance was mandatory.

"Maybe I'll even let you wear yellow," Maya jokes, without knowing how foreboding her words actually were.

A traffic light party is your typical off-campus get together, except that everyone is dressed in either red, yellow, or green depending upon their level of availability. Those people who were completely single and looking to score wear green, while their coupled and committed friends wear red. The yellows in the crowd represent those people who might be persuaded to go home with someone if the circumstances were right but are otherwise spoken for.

Maya and I wear red, and we are one of only two red couples in the place. The other reds are Leslie and Sue, a nice lesbian couple everyone is rooting for. In general, the room is a whirlpool of green sex hormones, and I look on with envy.

I bring Maya a Cougar Light, and she looks at it and then me with repulsion. The hosts didn't splurge for any kind of decent beer, which I don't mind because there is no cover charge and free drinks are, after all, free. Still, Maya decides to stick it out sober, and that means that I, too, will be boring. I hand off our beers to Silverstein, who will be double-fisting alcoholic beverages either until he convinces a girl to get with him or he becomes incontinent—or both. If there were a color more free than green, he'd be wearing it.

For the next few hours we chat with our peers much like the middle aged pass time with theirs. We even cover the same topics: family, future plans, television, and sports. I find myself dozing off every few minutes into a fantasy land of sorts. I imagine that Maya is not with me and that my shirt is not red. My eyes dart around the room like some android bent on inseminating the entire female population. Guy, red shirt, guy, GREEN—I stop for analysis. Looks: 8.8 out of 10. High marks for one of Dave and Robbie's friends (What does that say about me, I wonder.). Personality: N/A. Accessibility: Unknown. Inconclusive report; I'll have to go in for a more in-depth investigation. It goes on like this for as long as I can muster the strength to simultaneously ignore the people I'm taking to and still seem like I'm engaged in their conversation. Usually, some nods and "Mm hmms" buys me a few moments.

Flash—I'm back in reality, standing next to Maya, talking to Dave about his most recent battle with toe fungus. Really. I wouldn't even make this up.

"Get some fuckin' flip-flops. Jesus!"

My outburst is muted by the played out hip-hop polluting everyone's ears, but I know Maya picks up on my discontent. She waits for an opportune time to ask me if I want to leave.

"No, I'm okay."

"Are you sure?" She kisses me on the mouth before I can answer.

"Yeah, I'm having fun."

I haven't fooled her, but my weak persuasion skills have, for the time being, appeased her desire to tend to my needs. It's a weird game couples play.

After this conversation, I notice D.A. schmoozing it up with two not-so-bad looking greens. At least one of them is clearly flirting with him despite his yellow shirt indication of 'proceed with caution.' He wears yellow because he thinks it provides intrigue. Why does this guy wear yellow, yet stand alone? Who does he have waiting at home for him? Am I worthy of going through the light with him?

I'm proud of D.A. He's quite ordinary, but he's a good guy and a friend of mine. I know that if ever I need someone to talk to, or someone to do me a sincere favor, he'd be there for me. I'm glad that his good looks afford him as much womanly company as he desires. This opinion might be altered if we were in competition, but more likely than not, we'd be in cooperation, being each others wingman, and the second girl talking to him would have someone to flirt with as well.

Gilbert approaches Maya and me and gives Maya a kiss on each cheek.

"Where's my European greeting?"

I know it's wrong, but I need to pick on someone, and Gilbert is a perfect candidate. I shouldn't be surprised, though, when he proceeds to kiss me on both cheeks. I do my best to show that I don't mind; he's the one who's phobic, *hetero*phobic, I try to show.

"Where's Victor?"

I knew that whether I asked or not, he is going to tell us anyway, so I figure that I may as well show that I care enough to ask even though I'd truly rather not hear about it.

"He's off making out with some girl, probably." The way Gilbert says this is so over-the-top flamboyant that I have to stifle a laugh.

"Is he bisexual?" Asks Maya in a very concerned manner.

"He's just—" Gilbert pauses for effect. "Confused."

"He's not out of the closet?"

"Well he was two nights ago, but it seems that he has left his balls in there, and he had to go in to fish them out."

"Poor baby," Maya says as she reaches out to Gilbert for a hug.

Oh, what the hell. I join in to make it a group hug. I've always enjoyed group hugs, but to be honest, without any alcohol in my system, it felt pretty awkward.

Then it happens. That Girl walks in by herself, and she is a *green*. Where are the jocks she usually hangs out with? Who does she know at this party? I didn't see her on the invite list. Maybe she's just lost, stumbled into this apartment by mistake, and the green wife-beater is just a coincidence. No. It can't be. This interaction is fate, I decide.

I watch That Girl very closely as Maya consoles Gilbert behind me. She comes into the center of room kind of timidly, which is not what I'm used to seeing from That Girl. The image of her in my mind is one of pure confidence, and why not? She has every reason to be confident. I dream about her often, which I suppose makes her the girl of my dreams—and judging from the looks from green men around the party, I assume I'm not alone.

I sigh and close my eyes when I realize that it *is* fate, just not in the way I had imagined. This is a cruel joke God is playing on me. There is no other explanation. Why else would she be at the same party as me for the first time in my life when 1. I was literally bound to Maya (she has had my left hand gripped tight in hers ever since the group hug), 2. I am completely sober and therefore wouldn't have the courage to approach her even if I were released from bondage, and 3. I would stand no chance even if I was released from bondage and found the courage to talk to her because of the insurmountable competition all around me.

I tell you now there was once a dream that was That Girl. It is no more.

I lie in bed, awake now. Not my bed. Her bed. Maya's bed. She's asleep, her head in my shoulder crevice. All I want to do is elbow her in the forehead with my other arm and wake her up, but something tells me that would be inappropriate.

I think back to earlier that evening. I try to picture myself lying in bed with That Girl. It's actually not that hard from my current vantage point. Maya and That Girl have roughly the same hair color and style, and everything else is either distorted at his angle or hidden beneath the covers.

Maya lets out one of her very distinguishable snorts, and the dream is dead, again.

It occurs to me that all this internal wondering is not only useless, but harmful. If I ever did manage to get with That Girl, I would grow tired, bored, and antsy as inevitably as I did with Maya. I know it's not the girl I become uninterested in, but rather the concept of the girl. It's a horrible occurrence, but it's not under my control and I refuse to apologize for it. In fact, when society is ready to apologize for imposing this feeling of guilt upon me, I will be all ears.

***

I decide to buy Maya an expensive bouquet of flowers. You may be wondering how a poor college student has the money to pay for expensive flowers, so I'll tell you.

Early sophomore year, I came upon a very fortunate turn of events. I never once could have imagined that receiving the words "See me," on a paper at the beginning of term could have directly led to an increase in spending money, but it turns out that Neuroscience professors work in mysterious ways. I won't bore you with the details of the paper's topic or even try to describe what the course, itself, was about. What I will tell you is that I had a decent understanding of the material, and I thought I wrote a pretty decent paper. Needless to say, I was somewhat alarmed when the professor called me into his office hours to discuss it. I can see the conversation unfolding in my mind.

"Hello, Professor Watkins."

He stirs abruptly, as if I woke up him up from a day dream which was about to unlock the secrets of the universe. My bad.

"Mr. Quibley. Come in."

I take the seat opposite him. His office cramped and discombobulated; definitely the habitat of a mad scientist. He's even got Einstein making a goofy face on the wall.

"If I misunderstood the assignment I'd—"

"You were right on, Matthew."

I make a silly confused face and hope that he knows clarification is in order.

"I want to talk to you about one paragraph in particular."

"Which one?"

"This one, the one circled toward the end there."

He tosses me a copy of my own paper and I read the circled paragraph. It's the paragraph that I thought might get me in trouble for being too far off topic. In this section, I make wild assumptions about neuroscience in general and take leaps of faith that I know are scientifically unproven. My heart races in anticipation of what will clearly be a stern talking to about the scientific method and how essential it is to respect it. I'm not up for this lecture. Jesus, I mean, I only signed up for this seminar because I heard this scatter-brained old man was an easy grader, and now I get a "See me" and chastisement.

"Sir, what I meant was only that—"

"It's brilliant."

"Excuse me?"

"The connections you have made and the possible implications of such intuitive excellence—"

He stops. He takes a deep breath as if he is reminding himself not to get too excited. Excited over what though? This man is clearly insane.

"I'd like you to work with me, as my research assistant."

Panic. Is he coming on to me?

"Oh, sir, no. I—"

"I insist."

"But Professor, I was just spitballing some ideas I've had. I mean, I'm a physics guy, not a neuroscient—" I'm speaking clumsily now. "I really don't know anything about—"

"The issues you have raised, and the hypotheses you have set forth about the intricacies of the relationship between the build up of amyloid plaques in the nucleus basalis of Meynert and the proteoglycans and their causation of degenerative neuronal tissue, Matthew, it is some of the most innovative thinking I have ever come across. Quite frankly, I'm jealous I didn't think of it myself. I say, I've thought about these issues, clearly, but never exactly in this way. I don't think anyone has. There are some potentially profound implications here, young sir."

I had no idea. Seriously.

He stares at me, waiting for some sign of encouragement that I am just not prepared to give. He actually bought my mad writings? Of course he did; he's a mad scientist.

"I intend to research this topic with my team, Matthew, and I want you there to supervise. After all, it is *your* idea, and it will be *your* work."

No it won't; How can it be when I don't even know what the hell we're talking about?

"I really don't have too much time right now. My schedule is pretty full."

Full of womanizing, drunkenness, and playing video games.

"Your obligations are as minimal as you'd like them to be. I just want you on board so that I can research this area of vast potential with a clear conscience."

He's worried about plagiarism? Is that it? I'm about to tell him not to fret over it, that I couldn't care less if he pursues this idea of mine, that I'll sign over any intellectual property rights to him when he goes and changes the whole negotiating process with a simple offer.

"I'll pay you. There are stipends for this sort of thing, and you'll be published by the year's end! How many undergraduates can say that?"

Publish schmublish. How much money are we talking?

"What kind of stipends are granted to research assistants?"

I know I sound shallow, but let's face it: he seems to think that he needs me involved in this project, and I've got nothing to lose (except perhaps my dignity).

"$2,000 per term, I believe."

That would nearly double my funds.

"And you say my involvement can be minimal? Because I'm really busy with—"

"All I ask, son, is that you come chat with me for half an hour a week, any time you like. Of course you can contribute as much as you'd like, but at the very least, I'd like to have the opportunity to get your input on a weekly basis."

"Sounds fair. You've got yourself a research assistant."

Bam. $2,000 richer for doing next to nothing.

Flash back to present day. I feel rich and also a little guilty about pursuing Tangent X in secret so I purchase the flowers for Maya and hope that somehow this offsets my woeful actions. Now that *that's* done, I can focus on the task at hand: how to get together with Tangent X without risking being caught by Maya, or Molly, or anyone who might know any of us in any way.

It's Sunday night which actually turns out to be pretty convenient. Maya works at the library until it closes on Sundays, and it being a school night means that I can ask Tangent X if she wants to stay in and watch a movie in her apartment without sounding too lame. She seems receptive to the idea.

So I pick out a couple of DVDs and pick up a bottle of wine on my way to her place. When at the liquor store, I go with a bottle of pinot grigio. At first I thought about a white zinfindel, because to me it's the least offensive tasting wine around, but then I remembered what my mother told me about white zin (that it's a real non-drinkers drink), and I knew I had to change my purchase. I couldn't let Tangent X, my would be mistress, see me as a real non-drinker.

I arrive and she greets me with a smile and takes the bottle of wine from me.

"I brought two movies. We can watch whichever you want."

She takes my hand and sits me down on a sofa in the living room. If we were going out, I'd swear she was about to break up with me.

"Matt." She looks down and then back up at me. "I don't usually do what we did on Friday."

What did we do on Friday night? Silverstein tells me we made out on the dance floor. Was there more? Did we do anything that she might regret? I doubt it.

"What is it, exactly, that you don't usually do?"

She's horrified with embarrassment.

"You know. Don't make me say it."

Oh dear God. My mistress is a prude.

"Oh, that, yeah. Don't worry about that. I don't do that either, usually."

"Okay, good. So you're not expecting, *ya know*—I mean, I just didn't want you to think that I was easy or something."

I smile and put a hand on her knee (that's not going too far, is it?).

"Don't worry, really. I would never think that."

"Okay, good. Cause I've had my eye on you for a little while, and I can sort of see myself liking you," she pauses. "A lot."

Okay, I'm a little freaked out, but I'm not going to let her see that. If I play my cards right, I think I can use this to my advantage and have her bra off by the end of the night.

It turns out, my game is weaker than I made it out to be. Tangent X and I watched *both* movies, and I still didn't manage to get any more than a good night kiss and some nice conversation from her. To be honest, though, I'm not as annoyed by these results as you might think. Just getting to know Tangent X, doing the whole puppy-love introductory phase thing again, made the night pretty enjoyable. I'm actually very much looking forward to our next get-together.

***

Some weeks have passed now, and managing dual-relationships has turned out to be very doable, to my surprise and delight. At first, I was petrified by fear. Fear that Maya and Tangent X's paths would cross and that my chance for happiness would be foiled. Fear that Silverstein would say something stupid and give away all my secrets. Fear that my conscience would get the best of me.

Luckily, none of those fears came to fruition. Maya and Tangent X live very full and distinct lives. Maya works like a dog in her pre-med classes, volunteers at EMS regularly, cooks for herself, and likes to party with her friends when she gets the chance. Tangent X strictly sticks to courses in mathematics and her apartment is closer to the sciences library (Maya prefers the main library on the green). She's on meal plan, and so far she's been quite content to commit our affairs together in the privacy of her apartment. The two ladies share no friends, no professors, and no real interests—except me.

And my involvement in the dual relationships is pretty manageable, to be honest. I'm helped by the fact that physics is a lot like understanding women, either you get it square away, and you can make it work for you, or you don't. Aside from my assignments and the occasional preparation for exam time, it doesn't impose itself too much on my life, a relationship I am grateful to have. It allows me to pursue other endeavors, like my research assistantship with the Mad Scientist (the commitments of which I've clocked at about 27 minutes per week), playing entire seasons in baseball video games, and now my dual relationships.

I've ceased thinking about Tangent X as someone whom provides pleasure and excitement on the side, because in truth it's all up front—or at least diagonally across from me to the right while Maya is diagonally across from me to the left. I treat them separately but equally. See, separate but equal has acquired an awful connotation because of all those reprehensible civil rights associations, but the label does apply under different circumstances. Think about it. Parents are always saying that they love all of their children equally, but surely they treat them differently because they are, after all, different human beings with different needs. Maya and Tangent X are not my children, but they both provide me with something equally valid, no matter how different they are to each other.

I feel more comfortable around Maya, and at first this concerned me because I thought it supported the mistress perception of what I'm doing. Eventually, though, I realized that *of course* I'm going to be more comfortable with Maya now because I've been with her God knows how long and I've only just met Tangent X. That's okay! One of the reasons I'm enjoying the company of Tangent X so much is that she represents the new and unknown, and this is a very valuable thing. I treat them differently, but equally well.

Earlier, when I told you that men should be able to be with as many women as they could 'handle' (remember the good connotation applied when using this word in this way), this is what I was talking about. I can perfectly handle Tangent X and Maya at the same time. Notice I switched their names around to be in reverse alphabetical and chronological order; don't for a second think that this was an accident.

I've been a good significant other to both of them and they me. So what's the problem? Sure, I feel a little guilty (damn you society!). And yes, I acknowledge that I have totally jettisoned the 'it's only allowed if it's not meaningful' logic, as my relationship with Tangent X *has* become something I'd be reluctant to abandon. But that's not what's really troubling me. The real kicker, the thorn in my side if you will, is that I think I can handle *more*. I'm doing so well with two women that I have decided it is my personal duty as an evolutionary man in a defeated man's world to test my limits.

You may think I'm getting greedy, but I have my reasons. The way I see it, I'm on a crusade. A crusade against denying human nature, against pretending to be someone your not, against womanizers who don't respect their victims, against the notion that a gut feeling is always wrong, and finally against that ancient prick who damaged the life of any good man who ever said "I do" to just one woman.

I'm at the dining hall, finishing off my 'crusade tirade' to Silverstein and D.A., when I make my final decision to expand my circle of love. I notice a girl sitting alone at a nearby table. I take note of this girl often because she is always alone, and I wonder why. She's a Goth girl, but that shouldn't matter; there are lots of Goth guys and girls around with whom she could associate. She's an attractive girl underneath all that dark make up and eye liner, and her clothes aren't particularly offensive, even if they are all black and plain. Maybe she has an obscene personality, but I don't get that sense from watching her eat. She carefully picks away at her food, quietly adjusting every nuance of the cafeteria products' imperfections until they're ready to be ingested. This is not the characteristic of a loudmouth or violent type. After all of this time, all of these cafeteria lunches, seeing her sad and alone, I decide that it is time to figure her out.

I try to announce my intentions to invite the Goth girl over, but D.A. is on a rant about how people with Turrets Syndrome should respectfully excuse themselves during wedding ceremonies, and I can't seem to get a word in.

"It's just common courtesy! If you know you're at risk for shouting out obscenities at the top of your lungs when the minister asks if anyone has any objections to the union, you should let yourself out of the room!"

"You're a discriminatory bastard, you know that D.A.?"

Silverstein doesn't care about the rights of people with Turrets Syndrome; he's just giving D.A. a hard time.

"And anyway, a lot of wedding services don't even have that part. Like Jewish services."

Now, I'm pretty sure I've been to Jewish services where they *do* say that line, but Silverstein's about to back D.A. into a corner, and I'm going to let him because this is how I get my jollies.

"Well that doesn't change the fact that—"

"What? You don't think Jews matter? Is that it?"

"No, it's just that—"

"No, I see what's going on. Ya know, D.A., I thought we were pals, but if you want to be anti-semitic, then—"

"Shut up, Silverstein! You know I'm not anti-sem—"

"You want me to wear a yellow arm band and stay within the confines of the quad with my Turrets Syndrome friends?"

"You don't have any Turrets Syndrome friends."

"We're not *all* discriminatory bastards, D.A. I judge a person by what's on the inside."

"Yeah, that'll be the day."

"Hey, Matty, tell this racist douche bag that I'm not talking to him until he apologizes for making me feel guilty for killing Christ."

"I never made you feel guilty for killing Christ!"

"But you think *I* killed Christ? Jesus!"

I've had enough by now, so I grab them by the ear lobes and they wince with pain and silence immediately.

"I'm going to go over to that table and invite the Goth girl to sit with us."

They look at me as if I just said I was going to ask the lady with the eye patch and the beard who manages the salad bar to marry me.

"She sits there, all alone, every day. I just want to see if she wants some company."

"Dude! I was just going to tell the story from last night," Silverstein protests.

"You still can; I'm sure she'll enjoy it."

I stand up and walk toward the Goth girl's table. She slowly turns her head toward me with a scared look on her face as my shadow hovers over her tray.

"Hey," I say with a smile.

She's really confused now, and she looks around to see if anyone's watching.

"How's it going? My name's Matt."

I reach out a hand, and tentatively she shakes it.

"I'm Gwyneth."

Gothic Gwyneth. Perfect.

"I was wondering Gwyneth, I mean, I see you eating alone a lot, and I was just wondering if maybe you wanted to sit with me and my friends, have some company, ya know?"

She looks at Silverstein and D.A. just as Silverstein throws a French fry into D.A.'s drink and raises his arm in triumph and then looks back at me.

"I don't like people very much. Thanks, though."

I'm not giving up that easily. This girl intrigues me; she seems *different* than other girls I've ever been acquainted with.

"You don't like any people? That's too bad."

"Just most people. But it's not too bad. The feeling's mutual."

"I find that hard to believe."

"You don't know me," she says matter-of-factly.

"I'd like to."

I half-smile and raise my eyebrows.

"Come sit with us for ten minutes, and if you still don't like us you can leave, and I won't protest."

She sits silently for a moment, fidgeting with the salt shaker.

"Why are you doing this?" She asks.

"Because I like the way you eat."

Well, that, and because I'd like to see you naked—but mostly because of the eating.

For some reason, the food line works, and she is on her way back to the table with me.

We sit down, and I introduce her to the guys. She seems strangely suspicious of new people. Maybe she was abandoned when she was young, or perhaps she has no immune system but instead of choosing to live her life in a bubble she must be completely isolated. Just theories.

Without hesitation, Silverstein launches into his regaling tale of debauchery and fool heartedness.

"I will now tell the story of last night. But you must know, this is no *ordinary* story. This is my story of Vagabondage. You ready for it?"

We all nod.

"So before the pajama party on Waterman, I pre-gamed at Dave's."

"Of the Dave and Robbie variety?"

"That's the one. So we get heavily liquored up—"

"How unusual," chimes in D.A.

"And head to the party. I'm in a beater, boxers, and my favorite sandals—that's important for later on."

We again nod with anticipation. Sounds like a typical Silverstein story so far.

"Within five minutes of getting to the party, I know it's going to be one of those nights because I find myself making out with this girl on the dance floor and I have no idea how that happened."

"Hold up," interjects Gothic Gwyneth. "You," she pauses for effect, "found yourself, without any personal effort or motive, making out with a random girl?"

"You've got it."

"Okay, just double checking."

Good, I think. Gothic Gwyneth is integrating herself into the group.

"So I decide before it's too late, I'm going to see if she wants to go back to her place."

"You mean before you pass out," I joke.

"Hold on, damn you. I'm getting to that."

The table groans in one of those 'I'm disgusted by you but I can't wait to hear what happens next' sort of ways.

"So I get this girl to take me back to her dorm. She's a sophomore, and she lives on the Pembroke quad. She leads me into her room, everything's going swell, when—"

D.A. sings the 'dun, DUN, **DON**,' music that plays in every old time movie ever made when something goes awfully wrong. Gothic Gwyneth smiles; I'm pretty sure she's enjoying the company.

"When she starts getting undressed, I begin to feel a little queasy, and I think I might be sick. I tell myself that I can tough it out, and it'll be okay, so I take my sandals off and try to continue, when it becomes increasingly evident that I can't tough it out, and everything will *not* be okay. Well, I didn't want to puke on her, so without saying a word, I sprint out of the room, down the hallway, and into the bathroom."

"God, this poor girl."

"Poor girl? I was the one who was sick! Anyway, so I'm squatting on a dirty bathroom floor with my head in the toilet when I pass out."

More groans.

"I have no idea how long I was out for, but it must have been a while because when I awoke my vomit had dried up."

In my head, I imagine Maya's lecture to Silverstein on the dangers of alcohol poisoning.

"Sorry for the graphic nature of the Vagabondage. I'm just telling the story the way it happened. So, I get up, and take a look at myself in the mirror, and there's puke all over my white tank top. Just looking at it made me kinda queasy so—"

"Oh, no."

He nods his head.

"I went and puked all over the last remaining clean stall."

"You bastard."

"It was then that I realized I could definitely *not* go back into that girl's room."

"Why not?" I ask.

"Think about it, Matty. Some random guy from a party asks to go back to your room, then runs out just as things are getting interesting and gets sick all over himself. Would you want him to come in some hours later and continue things?"

"Well I hardly ever bring guys back form parties so I really don't know."

He smiles patronizingly and continues.

"So, I decide to collect myself and head back home, but I realize two three things: 1. I'm barefoot; I left my sandals in her room, remember. 2. I'm still way too drunk to know where I am. 3. I couldn't even get into my room if I found it because I didn't have the key (I was in a beater and boxers) and you were out."

Thankfully he didn't say with whom.

"So what did you do?"

"I left the dorm, barefoot, covered in my own vomit, and looked around. I thought I saw the lights from Thayer Street so I began making my way down that direction because Thayer Street leads to all places."

"That poor girl," Gothic Gwyneth repeats.

"Just then, catastrophe strikes. As I approach Lima, I look at my watch. It's exactly 2AM."

Groans. Lima is a very posh, European style club. Everyone who goes is very well dressed and pretty stuck up about it. 2AM is when it closes and all the clubbers are forced out into the street.

"Within seconds, I'm surrounded by dozens of Eurotrashers smoking their fags and driving their Lamborghini's right to my humiliation."

Makes sense. After all, if you saw a tubby little man walking down the street at 2AM, in his underwear, covered in vomit, what would you think?

"Before I know it, whispers turn into blatant staring and name calling. If I weren't so drunk, maybe I'd have defended myself—"

A pause.

"And I certainly wouldn't have walked into the trash bin like I did. But I *was* still drunk, and so I decide to brush off their hurtful glances and immaturity and continue on my journey."

"Wise."

"Before I know it, I'm on Angell, and I realize that I know someone on Angell."

"Maya," I interject before he can elaborate upon who exactly Maya is in front of Gothic Gwyneth.

"Right. So I make my way to Maya's apartment, and she looks at me with disbelief and invites me in. I do my best to explain my situation, that really I just need a place to crash for a few hours, and she says that she's not sure she can help me. She says that Gilbert'll probably be out for a little while longer, and that he probably wouldn't mind terribly if I took a nap in his bed until he came back. So without really thinking about it, I take her up on this offer and make my way to Gilbert's bedroom. I decide that it wouldn't be very considerate of me to get into Gilbert's bed wearing these clothes soiled in vomit and bathroom floor gooey-ness. So I strip."

"Excuse me?"

"I get naked, and slip into his bed."

"Oh, okay. Just making sure I heard you correctly."

"Yeah. So I spontaneously wake up some time later with a heart-wrenching, gut-twisting, die-just-at-the-thought-of-it fear. It occurs to me that I am lying naked in Gilbert's bed." He repeats, louder. "I AM LYING NAKED IN GILBERT'S BED!"

The entire cafeteria looks at him quizzically.

"This is not a good idea, I decide."

"What'd you think he was going to take advantage of you?" D.A. asks with a laugh.

"It was a wild night. I was not about to risk my anal virginity so that Gilbert could have his fun."

"You homophobic twit," I comment.

"Would you have risked it?"

"I wouldn't have been naked in Gilbert's bed to begin with!"

"Right, well anyway. I get out of there just as Gilbert arrives home with some guy, so I'm happy about that. And I make my way back to the dorm, where I proceed to curl up in a ball outside our door. Later that morning, Joe found me."

"The janitor?"

"Custodian, yes."

"So you were worried about Gilbert, but not Joe?"

"That's right. Joe and I are boys. He got the master key and let me into our room."

"Fair enough."

"But the thing that sucks is that after all that, I realized that I lost my best pair of sandals."

"Why don't you go back to the girl's room and ask for them back?"

"I couldn't do that."

Silverstein? Embarrassed? Whoa.

"C'mon. Where does she live? I'll do it."

"Would you? I bet she was so drunk she wouldn't even remember it was me and not you. You could pretend *you* were the one who ran out for no apparent reason and sicked all over the bathroom."

"Oh, can I? Can I please?"

Despite my facetiousness, I decided it would be fun, and I'd do it.

"What's her name?"

"Crystal. Crystal Herflagamy or something."

"Crystal Herschflagel? Oh my God. She was my freshman roommate!"

Gothic Gwyneth seems pretty excited for the first time ever.

"We hated each other. She used to tease me all the time about my clothes and stuff. So to get back at her I used to sleep with my boyfriend in front of her just to piss her off." She sighs. "Oh, memories."

Boyfriend? BOYFRIEND?

"Can I come too? I want to see the look on her face."

"Yeah, sure."

It'll give me an opportunity to investigate this boyfriend character.

After lunch I walk with Gothic Gwyneth across campus toward Crystal's dorm. I couldn't just come out and ask her if she is still with her freshman boyfriend because that would too obviously show my interest and with a fragile girl like GG, I was going to have to be crafty.

I find out some interesting tidbits about her on the way. She plays bass for a band and writes all of the music herself, but could never be lead singer because she couldn't stand having everyone stare at her on stage. I think it's an odd way to dress if you're looking to fit in but don't say anything. I ask her when her next show is and tell her that I'll be there. She also writes poetry, which I guess is similar to song writing, but never lets anyone read it. I tell her some day I will convince her to let me read it, and she thinks that this is funny. We focus mainly on getting to know her, and not me, but that's okay because I have a lot of questions and she seems happy enough that someone is finally curious enough to ask them.

She's from Westchester, New York, which I think is funny because I picture her stuck up parents and how they might sit around at dinner parties and tell their friends that "Gwyneth is only going through a phase right now with all that darkness and dreadful attire." They look forward to her days as an investment banker, I figure. Do the big investment firms hire Africana Studies majors? She tells me that she would have been a creative writing major but couldn't stand to have graders tearing her pieces to shreds, so she chose African Studies because it seems like the least reality-based area to study right now. Maybe she is going through a phase, I wonder. Otherwise, where will she be in ten years, when she can't run from reality anymore?

We arrive at Crystal's dorm and as we walk down her corridor I smell Silverstein's putrid vomit from the bathroom and am tempted to call the whole thing off. I see that he has left the bathroom completely and utterly unusable. This girl's been through enough, I figure. But Gothic Gwyneth urges me onward and we continue toward Crystal's room. I knock and open wait for an answer.

"Hi."

She looks at me and then does a double take at Gothic Gwyneth.

"Gwyneth, I haven't seen you since—"

"Freshman year, yeah. I was hoping never to see you again, but then you had to go and bring my boyfriend home last night. Big mistake."

She's altered the game plan spontaneously and I'm caught off-guard. Am I her boyfriend in this scenario? And if so, does that mean she is, in reality, single? She really wants to make Crystal uncomfortable, which I'm feeling a little awkward about, but I keep quiet for the time being. I'm looking pretty ashamed of what's going on, which probably only helps along Gothic Gwyneth's game. She continues to give the poor girl a hard time while Crystal desperately tries to recall the details of the previous night. She probably knows she went home with somebody, but doesn't remember the guy looking anything like me.

"Wait a second. I went home with a guy named, um—"

"Silverstein. Gwyneth's just joking around." I interject. The charade's up, and in fact, I decide to take it a step further and make this girl feel better about the whole situation.

"The reason we're here actually, is that our friend Silverstein, he left his sandals here last night. Actually this is a little embarrassing, but he did this because he really liked you and wanted an excuse to come back the next day."

"Oh."

She's confused, but it looks like she's buying the story.

"So why didn't he come back himself? Wouldn't that be the point?"

Damn. That *would* be the point if it were actually the reason he left his sandals there.

"Well, yeah, but—"

I'm stumped and clearly in trouble when Gothic Gwyneth comes to the rescue.

"He realized that you'd see right through the act, and he was a little too embarrassed to go through with it."

"Right! But he really does need those sandals back, and we were heading in this direction, so we said we'd pick them up for him."

"Oh, okay. Well, here you go."

She picks up the sandals and hands them to us. With a smile (authentic from me and sinister from GG), we're off.

We've got Silverstein's sandals back, and this girl comes away thinking she has an admirer who's too smitten to even come by. God bless, I figure.

***

I've been handling three women pretty well, if I do say so myself—though technically Gothic Gwyneth shouldn't be included because we haven't *done* anything. Nevertheless, things are progressing nicely with her. I went to see one of her shows and was unexpectedly impressed. The lead singer kept shooting me dirty looks, and I couldn't tell if it was because I stood out like a sore thumb in my modern hipster attire or what. Her band, Krimson with a K, doesn't play the type of music I anticipated they would. I had thought that it would be full of screaming and heavy distortion, when in reality the music is quite melancholy and brooding, ala Elliot Smith before he killed himself. Hmm. That's a little worrisome, now that I think about it. But what can ya do? I like to think that I'm pretty perceptive about people, and Gothic Gwyneth does *not* seem like the type of person who would do herself in—too stubborn.

Tangent X and I are moving along quite nicely. We've transitioned into that phase of a relationship where you're no longer kept up at night with excitement, but you're definitely still enjoying the adventures of exploring new experiences with each other—I won't get into gory detail. I've grown to really enjoy her personality, too. She views everything logically, which I like. I feel like she's above the bullshit a lot of the time. Like I don't have to pretend that I'm someone I'm not. She never asks me what I'm thinking, and so I never have to make up some convoluted reply.

But I'd hate to give you the impression that I was in some way trying to show you how these girls have given me something that Maya never could; Maya still contributes more per capita than any of the others, I'd say. Because she's the one I know the best, she's the one I can still talk to, really talk to. She's also got an intuitiveness about me that the others haven't picked up yet. Maybe they never will. I'm not sure. I know that I have to be careful because even though I think I'm doing well handling three women, a little slip up in front of Maya and the jig'll be up—no doubt about that. This weekend will be my first big challenge.

Maya's great aunt died, and I'm driving to her home in New York for the funeral. I met her aunt once, nice old lady, and I know Maya would be in no condition to travel alone. She takes death very seriously, as I suppose it's intended to be taken.

We once had a conversation about why we wanted to be what we wanted to be. It went something like this.

"Why do you want to be a physicist?"

"I'm good at the material. I think I could be a star in the field, that sort of thing."

"But you're good at a lot of things. You're the best Pinball player I've ever seen. Why don't you train to be a professional Pinball player?"

"They don't exist."

"But you would if they did?"

"Maybe, depends on the pay."

"That's disgusting."

"Not really. How is it any different from being a professional baseball player?"

"Well, at least professional baseball players can give back to their communities and donate money to charities if they wanted."

"If I were good enough at Minesweeper to make millions of dollars, maybe I'd donate most of it to charity, too."

"Fine."

"Well, what about you? You think you're doing something so high and mighty by training to be a doctor?"

"If I'm a doctor, I could conceivably save the lives of thousands of people. Lots of people will live longer because I treated them, and that, to me, means something."

"You think if you weren't there, those patients would just wither away and die? You don't think they'd find another doctor?"

"Your logic is flawed, Matt. It's the dilemma of the commons. If all the doctors thought the way you do, there'd be no doctors and no one would get treated."

"But if you're so keen on helping people, why don't you go to Africa, volunteer for one of those international medical organizations."

"There you go again. If all doctors thought that way, no one would be here to help you."

I laugh.

"So you're doing it for me, then?"

"People like you."

"Now it's you who has got the flawed logic, lady. It's because everybody thinks the way *you* do that there aren't enough doctors in places like sub-Saharan Africa."

"Wrong again. You're forgetting about a million other factors: economics, finances, cultural climate and issues of security. These are all issues that limit the do-gooders from doing good."

"Okay, whatever."

We sit in silence for a minute before she concludes.

"Death, as I see it, is the worst possible thing that can happen to a person."

"What about torture?"

"Well, if you survive the torture, you're that much stronger from it, aren't you?"

"I guess."

"If you die, that's it. You're done. A lot of people think you'll be able to watch over as your family grieves, that you'll be able to hover over everyone and watch as the world continues without you—and I can't definitively say that that doesn't happen—but it's certainly not the feeling I get. I think that death is nonexistence and that alone. Just a dreamless sleep from which you never awaken. So if I can help people prevent death, or at least postpone it in my professional life, then I think that's a worthy cause."

Needless to say, I knew she would be pretty perturbed when she found out about her great aunt. When she told me over the phone, I rushed over to her apartment and hugged her. We were locked in an embrace for something like twenty minutes, when I told her that I would drive her home and attend the funeral with her if she'd let me. Through some sobs, she agreed.

I told Tangent X that a friend's aunt has passed away, and I'm giving her a lift home. This is a white lie because although Maya *is* a friend, that's not the whole story, obviously as you know, but I decide that it's acceptable under these circumstances, considering all of the crappier atrocities I've committed over the past few weeks.

I'm still too early in the relationship with Gothic Gwyneth to have to explain my absence for the weekend. I do make plans to get together with her upon my return, however. I know she wouldn't be up for the typical date stuff (e.g. dinner and a movie, ice skating downtown, etc.) so I tell her that I haven't figured it out yet but that we'll do something more fun than she's expecting. I still can't tell if she likes me or if she just enjoys having someone's attention. It doesn't really matter to me at this point; I like having her company regardless.

The car ride is pretty brutal, but I think I do alright as the supportive boyfriend. I ask Maya if she wants to talk about things, and she doesn't. I wonder if I'm supposed to prod her to explore her feelings, but I decide that I shouldn't. I'm no therapist. If she wants to talk, she knows I'm here to listen and hug. Those are pretty much the two job requirements for the Consoling Boyfriend.

She cries a little, so I offer my right hand. It's the best I can do while I'm driving, I figure.

When we get to her home, her parents take over the comforting duties, and I'm welcomed like a hero coming back from battle.

"It was really great of you to do this," Maya's father, the rabbi, says as he embraces me.

"Don't mention it. I'm really sorry for your loss."

"You're a sweet boy, Matthew. I'm very glad for Maya to have someone like you in her life."

I'm swine. If only you knew, sir.

"Maya's a very special girl. I'm lucky to have her in mine."

This is true, and it feels like it's the first time in weeks that I don't have a knot in my throat as I speak.

The funeral is a short but moving graveside ceremony. I'm surprised to find myself shedding a few tears in the great aunt's honor, even though I only met her once. I get caught up sometimes when people around me are crying, and I can't help but let my eyes water.

On the ride back up to school, I let Maya know that I'm going to be relatively busy this week. She asks me to elaborate, and I make up something about a physics project and some extra hours with the Mad Scientist. I'm not sure how natural I sound. Sometimes she looks at me like she can see through my facade and read my thoughts, but I figure this perception must be in my head because if she could read thoughts she'd be a psychic, and then she'd already know what I had been doing and she'd have dumped me a long time ago. No, she can't read my thoughts.

We get back to school around at around 10PM, and I hug her and begin to say good night. I had snuck in a text to Tangent X earlier in the day saying that I wanted to see her when I got back that night. Maya wasn't having any of it.

"You're going?"

"Yeah, I figured that it's been a long day and you probably just wanted to rest."

"I can rest with you here. Can you stay?"

I try to mask my hesitation, probably unsuccessfully.

"Sure. I'll stay."

I sneak into the bathroom and text Tangent X an excuse why I can't come over tonight, and then immediately erase the text from my cell phone's memory.

Within an hour, Maya is asleep in my arms, and I am miserable. It's not supposed to feel this way, I think. This moment is tender by all notions of sensitivity I've ever had. How come I'm suffocated by a desire to leave, then?

Of course I don't leave. I stay the night and get about two hours of sleep before a meeting with the Mad Scientist.

The trouble with my recent meetings with the Mad Scientist is that our research—his research—has become too advanced for me to understand. I realize now that the Mad Scientist never wanted me on board with the project as a supervisor at all. I suppose I saw that from the beginning, but it's all too clear now. Originally he asked me on board to clear his conscience, so that he could investigate my hypotheses without thinking that he was stealing my ideas. Now though, I think he enjoys our meetings because he is able to explain to me how he's making great strides toward helping the world. Since week two, he has been convinced that he is on the verge of some brilliant discovery that's going to revolutionize the field. I highly doubt it will happen, but I'm happy to listen to his rants for $2,000 a term.

This week, however, I don't have the patience for his nonsense. As soon as he starts with his research updates, I stop him. I apologize to him because I feel bad; I am no longer able to understand half of what he says about the research and I'd be patronizing him to pretend that it really interested me because he and I both know that half of what he says is gibberish to me.

"Are you alright, son? You don't seem well. Are you ill?"

"No, I'm not ill. I'm okay."

"Are you sure? If you'd like, we can reschedule this meeting for when you're feeling up to it."

"No, no. I'm fine, really."

Without warning, a sudden urge comes over me. I want the Mad Scientist's perspective regarding my assault on modern day monogamy.

"Do you mind if I ask you a personal question, sir?"

He looks at me as though I've asked to rummage through his underwear drawer, which I guess isn't too far from the truth from the Mad Scientist's viewpoint.

"Um, I suppose that would be fine."

"Don't worry, Professor. I won't pry."

He flashes a smile of relief.

"Have you ever been in love?"

"Love," he balks, "is that what you want to ask me about?"

I nod.

"The only love I know is for my work."

He pauses thoughtfully.

"Friends, lovers, family members, they all come and go. You and your work are the only constants in your life. You and your work are the only variables that can't let you down, that you have control over."

That may be the saddest thing I've ever heard, but I nod approvingly.

"What are you really asking about? Sex?"

Oh my God. The old man, the Mad Scientist, just asked me about sex. I blush.

"It's okay son. It's there. There's a giant elephant in the room, and do you know what? He's wearing a thong! There's no point in ignoring it."

Excuse me while I vomit a little bit.

"I used to do my best to abstain from sexual activities. I looked upon sex like a scientist should. And since I have no desire to procreate any further, there was no reason I should be ruled by a remnant of our evolutionary desires and societal reinforcements."

"Talk to me about societal reinforcements, if you don't mind."

"You've heard it all before, I'm sure. Ask yourself why people are sexually driven aside from the underlying desire to pass on their genetic code."

"Because it's fun, and—"

"No. It is fun because we're programmed to think it's fun. If you can overcome the evolutionary basis for spreading your seed, the only factors remaining are those of societal influence. All your friends are interested in broads, so you are, too."

Broads? I barely hold in a snicker.

"Movies, television, books, your friends, your parents, all of these influences tell you that you should be physically attracted to women."

But all of those same societal factors also tell me to be faithful to my girlfriend, right? Or maybe they have painted a picture of how a man's supposed to act and in that schema the man is a lying, cheating bastard.

"Imagine for a moment, Matthew, that you live in ancient Rome. You would probably not only be my pupil, but also my lover!"

Oh no. Please strike me dead and allow this conversation to be over.

"How's that?" I ask, not really wanting to know the answer.

"Before the Roman Catholic Church came to prominence, sexuality was viewed in a much different manner. Our modern notions of homosexuality and monogamy were quite foreign to the ancient Romans. *Their* society reinforced a policy of openness."

"I don't understand. Were all Romans bisexual?"

He balks.

"No! That's exactly the point! The environment around you has such a powerful impact upon your behavior that it can make anything seem like the 'right' course of action, as if there were such a thing. There are a thousand examples just like that. I'm sure you've come across the interesting tidbit that some six hundred years ago the most attractive women were the ones who would be considered obese by modern standards."

"Right, right. I have heard about that. It's because they were perceived to be wealthy enough to have an abundance of food high in fat content."

"Yes. So you see, there are no absolutes when it comes to sexual attraction. What is right or wrong for one person in one era is completely foreign to another person who is the product of a different environment."

I see what he's getting at now, but I'm not at all sure how it helps my situation.

"In my youth, I tried to be above the influence of evolutionary urges and societal influences," he continues. "And so for some time I was celibate. It didn't last long. It's a fundamental flaw in man; you know the old saying, we've been given the gifts of both the brain and the genitalia, but only enough blood to have one functioning at a time."

Don't say genitalia, again. Please.

"Now, I shag whenever the urge strikes me, assuming I have the funds."

"You pay for it?"

"Of course! Who would want to shag an old nut like me for free?"

I nod in agreement and thank him for his candid response. A part of me wishes I had just stuck to neuroscience, but now he's got me thinking. How does what the Mad Scientist said relate to my dilemma? I do wish to procreate, but not yet—God forbid. The old man said that none of us are really above the urges and influences, and I am certainly not. Nor do I want to be. I *like* not being above them; it's fun. You probably think I'm some sort of womanizing fishmonger, but I'm not. I love women. I love them so much that I can't limit myself to just one. Why would I want to rid myself of that feeling?

So what's the answer for me? The Mad Scientist has convinced me that there are no rights or wrongs when viewing these issues from an analytical perspective. My conscience begs to differ, but what does it know? It's apparently just a product of my upbringing in a society which advocates for commitment. Or is it? Is there no such thing as an innate moral code by which we're meant to live? I should have asked the rabbi when I had the chance.

A knock on the door. I'm in bed in my dorm room, and I can't imagine who in the world would be knocking on my door at this hour. I mean, it's not even—okay, so it's past noon, but still, it's Sunday, the day of rest for me, anyway. I look over at Silverstein's bed and see that he's out cold, unshaken by the knocking which is growing louder by the second. I jump out of bed, make my way toward the door, and open it.

It's That Girl. God, she looks great. How can anyone be so perfectly perky after a Saturday night? Oh, and there's some guy with her, too. She greets me with a smile, which is about when I realize that I'm in my underwear. I reposition my posture to conceal any lingering morning wood—though of course they don't know my intentions so to them it looks like I'm just struggling through the pains of a hernia or something.

"Hope we didn't wake you."

"No, no. I was just, um, sleeping."

Not the quickest in the morning, I admit.

"Don't worry about it, I meant to get up hours ago."

"Oh, okay, great. Would you mind signing our petition then?"

She hands me a sheet of paper filled with signatures.

"Chad and I are trying to reverse the cut in exercise facility funding for the spring."

Exercise facility funding? I mean, of all the causes to wake up for on a Sunday morning—Jeez. To be honest, though, if she'd been pushing a petition to secede from the Union I'd probably have signed it.

"Sure, sure. Yeah, I think I've seen you around the gym a bunch," I say to That Girl.

"We practically live there."

When I want your input, I'll let you know, Chad.

I smile and sign the petition.

"You want my phone number too?"

"I'm sorry?"

She looks at me like I'm out of my skull. She didn't take it as an innuendo as hoped, so I have to back peddle and try to save face.

"Oh, sorry. Some other petitions I've done require contact info."

"Oh, yeah. That's okay!"

Chipper and perfect—excuse me while I adjust my posture again. She's really something else.

"Okay, well thanks a lot. We better be moving along. Still need to get to all of the West Campus dorms after this."

I smile and watch them walk away and proceed to bang my forehead against the door for three minutes. Could I have been more ordinary, less notable, other than the fact that I was still sleeping in the afternoon and answered the door in my skivvies? It could have been worse, I guess. Silverstein could have answered the door; he sleeps in the buck.

I decide to take Gothic Gwyneth to the rooftop of the Prominence Hotel, our city's best attempt at a sky scraper. I know someone who works there, and I happen to know the view from the rooftop is pretty surreal.

"You better not have booked a room for us," she says in the elevator.

I laugh even though I can't tell if I should take her seriously. Regardless, I try to convince her that my intentions are more gentlemanly than she implied. When we get to the penthouse my buddy Chip leads us up to the balcony. I thank him and he's on his way. Gothic Gwyneth runs toward the balcony's edge and looks down at Kennedy Plaza below. It's a maelstrom of activity, but it seems as distant and serene as the television does when you've fallen asleep on the couch with it on.

The sun is setting and the sky screams all kinds of hues that only an artist could describe. Gothic Gywneth even seems moved.

"So there are colors other than black."

Why did I say that? She'll think I'm picking a fight with her, when all I wanted to do is make her smile. She opens her mouth to make fun of my collared shirt, probably, but I stop her by touching my lips to hers. Don't let go, Matty. As soon as you do she'll really let you have it.

She pulls back and looks into my eyes, not with the horror and anger which I imagined, but rather intrigue.

"You're not going to throw me off the balcony?"

"Nope. Lizard might though."

"Who the hell is Lizard?"

"My exboyfriend."

It's the lead singer of her band. Jesus. She went out with him? Is it rude to ask if she's ever been tested?

"Has he ever killed anyone before?" I joke.

"Never convicted."

Please, please, please let her be kidding, too. She smiles at me; okay, she is. Breathe, Matt, breathe. She takes a pack of cigarettes and a lighter out of her cargo pocket, cuffs her hand around the struggling flame, and lights one up. I stare at her as she gazes out toward the sky.

"Lemme guess. You've never smoked one."

"Not since the seventh grade. Why, is that your first?"

She laughs, good.

"They got me hooked at rehab. Ironic, eh? It's not that they're against drugs, just the ones that arbitrarily aren't allowed by the government."

I'm not sure how respond to this liberal hippy rationale, and she sees me going through the usual series of contemplations right in front of her and probably thinks I'm being rude even though I haven't said anything.

"Oh, didn't you know you were courting a nut case?"

"I had a feeling, but I thought you were courting me."
She laughs at me.
"Can you guess what else is wrong with me?" She asks.
"Don't they tell you not to talk like that?"
"Who?"
"The voices in your head."
I pause for laughter that doesn't come. Oh jeez.
"No, you know, therapists and counselors and the such."
"Oh, yeah. But what do they know?"
"Don't know. Never been to one."
"You're avoiding my question."
"What question?"
"What else is wrong with me? There are three others, besides drug addiction. I bet you can guess them."
"I don't want to play this game."
"C'mon, Matt. It's easy."
I still hesitate. I'm no shrink. It's not my job to diagnose.
"How's this," she proposes. "I'll name four undesirable psychological disorders and you name the one that I don't have."
How hard can this be? I agree to do it.
"Major depression."
"Check."
"Wait 'til I've named all four, dummy."
"Oh, sorry."
"Major depression, OCD, borderline personality disorder, and—"
She pauses and looks up at the sky.
"Murder-Your-Boyfriend-In-His-Sleepitis."
I smile and say that I don't know; it seems like she probably has all four. She flicks her cigarette over the ledge and tells me that she has been fighting bouts of depression since age fourteen, has had OCD since age six, and she's not really sure what borderline personality disorder is but that her shrink diagnosed her last year.

"How come I never notice the OCD, except with your food, anyway?"

"You really don't?"

I shake my head.

"I must be getting better at hiding it. I used to do all sorts of things that I've learned to control. Flicking light switches on and off three times every time I walk into a room. Always walking on the left side of people, unless there are three of us, in which case always walking on the far right side. Avoiding every fifth stair. That sort of thing."

"Sounds exhausting."

"It is. But that's what you get when you're a nutcase."

Why do I find it so attractive that this girl is so fragile? It doesn't make sense. Is it that Maya's so strong and unwavering, and anything opposite to Maya fills some void for me? I don't know.

"Isn't it all a little cliché?"

"Isn't what a little cliché?"

"Being depressed and being Goth."

"I don't think so. I was depressed before it was cool to *look* depressed, so I can dress however I want I figure."

I have a severe crush on this sad, sad girl.

"Do you want to get a room?" She asks.

"A room, a room here? What do you mean, exactly?"

"Well, it's too dirty to screw up here on the balcony, isn't it? And someone might see us."

Um. Okay. Don't hyperventilate, Matt. What is the proper course of action here? Handle, handle, *handle* it well. Do the right thing. Don't take advantage of her. She's only doing this because she has low self-esteem. Don't reject her. Maybe reject her, but don't make her *feel* rejected. Make it seem like she's rejecting you. How the hell can I do that? Damn it.

"Well?"

I can't. I've got the clap.

I wish I could, but I can't. You're on your period.

I'm impotent.
I'm allergic to sex.
I don't have protection.
I don't have sex organs.
I don't have money.
"Um."

She laughs. 'Um.' That's what I went with. Jeez. It's a miracle I can *handle* one woman with my communication skills.

"It's okay, Matt. I'm not about to jump off the fuckin' ledge because you feel guilty about having sex on the first non-date."

"Oh, okay. Good."

"Prude."

We laugh, embrace, and kiss atop the most romantic site in all of college town.

***

For about two weeks, I did fairly well with three girls. Maya's been a little suspicious that something's up, but I'm pretty sure she's too busy with organic chemistry to really worry about it. I'll shower her with attention and gifts as soon as she finishes with her midterm, and that should take care of that.

I've come to an important realization, and I thought it to be an appropriate time to share it with you. On the grand spectrum of handle-ability, I score pretty well: a five. It is my honest opinion that I can handle five women, and this makes me happy. Five? You may be wondering how I arrived at that number since I've only described my affairs with three: Maya, Tangent X, and Gothic Gwyneth. Well, there have been progressions, and the number is up to five. I'm no braggart, though, so I'm not going to take you through all of the details of these last two like I did the first three. What's important to know is that the number is now five, and I'm happy. Add the names Teenybopper and Wait Staff to the list. It is now complete; there will be no more additions. I am not above my own limitations, and I know that five is as many girls as I can properly handle. Good.

Teenybopper is, you guessed it, a teenager. Don't gasp. You knew it was coming; you're not shocked. Silverstein believes that a girl never looks as good as she does when she's seventeen years old. Now, I don't believe that. But you have to admit that there is something positively enticing about the notion of dating a school girl. So innocent and pure. She's a sweet girl, really. I actually was hitting on her friend at the mall, outside the pretzel shop, but her friend seemed utterly uninterested. Just as I was about to walk away with my tail between my legs, Teenybopper approached me and told me not to feel bad, that her friend was just in a male-hating phase because her father cheated on her mother and I shouldn't take it personally. In fact, she said, a girl would be crazy to reject me. Swear to God, that's what she said. Well anyway, it was pretty easy from there to pursue a benign puppy love relationship with this girl. She's pretty easily smitten with the older guy aspect to me, so it really hasn't been hard to add her to the gang.

Wait Staff is another story. She works at that retro themed diner on Thayer Street, hence the name. I knew I had to have her the first time she waited on me. And before you get on me about the name, how about you just give me a break. I'm just not that creative and at least this one's not a teenager, right? See, all members of the wait staff draw something with mustard they dispense. She drew boobs, and she winked at me in a way that said, 'my breasts look like these, would you like to taste the real things?' The interesting thing about Wait Staff, though, is that she's a twenty eight year old vagabond, pretty much. But a cute vagabond. What I mean is that she's kind of homeless. When she's not working, she's playing guitar on the street with an open guitar case next to her for spare change. Also, she seems to reside permanently at the YMCA downtown. Now, I'm not saying that her grunginess is a turn on, but something about the picture I just painted for you certainly is. Maybe it's the age. For every reason that Teenybopper is an asset, Wait Staff represents an equally powerful but opposing tool in my arsenal of relationship happiness. She's quite significantly older than me. She's wild and experienced. In fact, she often makes me feel like I'm lucky to have the opportunity to learn from her, which is a rare quality I've found. Also, she doesn't require much time on my end, and at this point that's a very valuable quality.

The point is that the troop is complete now, and I'm proud of myself. I've done it. Sure, it's all a giant secret that's eating away at my insides and making me lose my mind, but I've done it in spite of all that. I'm living the dream, and that ancient loser who promised monogamy can go be happy with just one cavewoman because I'm not having any of it. I've got everything I need.

Maya. The base. The foundation. She's the key to everything. Without her, none of the others would stand on their own. She's everything I grew up looking for in a girl and more.

Tangent X. My first venture into handling multiple women. Rational and straight up. God bless her.

Gothic Gwyneth. The most intriguing of the bunch. Delightfully fragile. Incredibly creative and a surprisingly good conversationalist. Not surprisingly also a great kisser. An essential component.

And last Teenybopper and Wait Staff. The final pieces to the puzzle. Equally valuable and yet complete opposites. Providing two more necessary outlets for my evolutionary urges and societal influences (thanks Professor).

A perfect squad. Finally happiness. I think.

***

It's the weekend of the Fresher's Fayre when everything changes. It tends to be a weekend filled with wild stories and adventures, but I'm feeling a little tired and so I'm up in my room playing video games when I get The Call from D.A.

"Dude."

"Yo, what's up, player?"

"You gotta come down here."

"What, to the green?"

"Yeah."

"No, man. I'm in the middle of a game."

"No, I mean I gotta talk to you about something."

Guys never *have* to talk to you about something unless something is indeed up, so I agree to meet him down on the green in five minutes. When I get there, I can't find him, but I see Maya and Molly. I give Maya a kiss hello and I smell the alcohol on her breath—very unlike Maya. I tell her that I'm looking for D.A. Maya becomes frozen in some sort of panic that I don't understand right away, and Molly says that they don't know where he is.

I continue searching for D.A. and eventually find him toward the back of the green. I ask him what's up, and he sits me down. What the hell is going on? He tells me that he's not sure of anything, but that something is definitely *up*. I ask him what he means, and he tells me that he was taking a piss in one of the fraternity bathrooms when he overheard two girls talking. He wasn't paying any real attention to the conversation, and he certainly doesn't remember what was said. When he exited the bathroom he sees that the two voices are coming from Maya and Molly. Instead of the expected warm greeting, they looked back at him, horrified. He says he smiled and waved hello before walking out of the frat. On his way out he heard Molly ask, 'that bad?' and Maya reply, 'definitely.' That's it. That's all he knows.

"But what do you *think* they were talking about?"

"I really don't know, man. I'm sorry. I wish I had been paying attention. I just know that they were talking about something they didn't want me to hear, and they really seemed spooked to see me. Find Maya, that's my advice. Just ask her what the deal is."

"Yeah, but she's drunk."

"Doesn't matter, I'd say. You need to find out."

I thank him and put a hand on his shoulder. I go off in search of Maya and before I find her, she spots me. She approaches looking down at the ground.

"I found D.A." I say.

"What'd he have to say?"

"What do you have to say?" I reply.

"Matt, can we do this later or tomorrow? I really don't know if I'm up for this now."

Up for this. What is *this*.

"It's okay, Maya. I just want to talk to you."

She looks up at me and then back down at the ground, and I know what's coming. It makes me queasy, and I wish it were a dream—but it's not. My knees grow weak in the split second I'm waiting for her to confess.

"I kind of hooked up with someone."

That feeling of sickness only becomes more profound as its accompanied by rage. If I don't hit something, I'm going to burst.

"Say something, Matt. Please."

I want to say something, anything would do. But I can't. No words come, and even if they could my voice would be quivering. All I can do is shake my head and close my eyes as I suddenly feel exhausted, totally drained.

She reaches out to embrace me, at which point the anger returns, and I shake her off of me in a violent throw of my arms. She sees the hatred, now, and she's frightened.

I have to get out of here. Go back to the room, I tell myself. Escape.

I storm away from Maya and make my way back to the dorm, where I am disappointed to find my anger remains. I proceed to kick the shit out of a freshman for bumping into me in the halls and collapse on my bed.

***

So this is what depression is like. To be honest, it's not all that great. I haven't really got an appetite, so I don't eat, so I'm weak and ornery all the time. I stopped shaving and showering, too, so I look kind of like a homeless man. It doesn't help that I've regressed to urinating in various jugs and bottles which are lying around the room. I haven't taken any calls or IMs in a week, from anyone, not just Maya. Silverstein says she's real sorry and that she really just needs to talk to me. I tell him to fuck off, and he does. Ever since word got out that I beat up that freshman, everyone looks at me a little differently—like I'm an impostor, someone pretending to be Matthew Quibley. And that reminds me, I have a Dean's hearing for violent conduct in the dorms later today. I'm not sure if I'll go.

You think I'm overreacting. That's okay. You couldn't possibly understand. You don't know what it's like to wallow in discontent for your entire conscious existence only to see a glimpse of happiness and then watch it be taken from you for eternity. It's not even what Maya did, because God knows I've done worse. It's what the action represents that really gets me. I was wrong. I can't handle five women. I couldn't even handle the *foundation*, the key to everything—the one. It was all a mirage. A false hope. I should have seen it coming. I couldn't have been the first man to attempt a coup. And I certainly wasn't the first to fail. I'm back to square one now. No. Square one would have been having just one woman, Maya. I'm back to square zero. I've got nothing. I'm at rock bottom, and I can't even see the surface.

I've written Maya three emails and two letters and sent none of them. The last one read like this:

Maya, I hate you. You've ruined everything, you stupid slut. You just couldn't let me be happy, could you? Well, I have news for you. I've been screwing around with four other girls. You think you hurt me? Well take that and multiply it by four, and tell me how you feel. If I really wanted to hurt you I'd tell you who they were and how much they MEANT to me. I'd tell you that I LIKED them. But that's all over with now. I don't like anybody anymore, and I especially don't like you. So you want to know why I'm not returning your calls? It's because I couldn't stand to hear your stupid voice, okay? Is that good enough? Leave me alone. Goodbye. Matt

The other messages were quite similar. I do plan on eventually sending one, as soon as I can write one without all the blind hatred and name-calling. I wish to explain to her how I'm feeling, but right now I just can't find the appropriate words.

Silverstein says my Dad called, real angry and confused, saying that University called him about the Dean's hearing. He wants me to call him back. Well fuck that. I'll call him when I damn well please. But I guess I'd better go to the hearing, try to get this thing sorted out so I can go back to being a shadow. I can't very well do that if they kick me out of dorms and I have to live in a box on Thayer Street, I figure.

I make nice with the Dean and avoid any real punishment. I also apologize to the freshman whose ass I kicked. When I get back to my room, Silverstein and D.A. are waiting for me; apparently, they're staging an intervention.

"This has got to stop."

Silverstein points to the bottles of urine lining the walls.

"Oh, come on. It adds character to the room, don't you think D.A.?"

"We're worried about you, man. You gotta get a grip."

"I'm fine."

"You're Howard Hughes without the funds."

"Guys seriously, I'm alright. I'm a little pissed at Maya for mucking everything up, but—"

"Whoa, right there, killer. You did this. You. Not Maya."

Look at D.A. being a tough guy.

"I treated her fine, man. Silverstein, you know. Tell him."

He shakes his head 'no.'

"I don't think she'd see it that way."

Silverstein calling me on something serious—things *must* be out of hand.

"Just give me some time to figure everything out."

"You've had enough time," shouts Silverstein.

D.A. claps his hands twice, and instantly an army of eight freshman storm into the room.

"What the fuck?"

I'm at a total loss as to what's about to happen to me, and to be honest, I'm a little frightened. As the eight frosh close in on me, I look to D.A. for help. He just shakes his head. Hands start grabbing at me, and before I know it my legs are swept right off the ground; I'm being carried somewhere. Out into the hallway. Down about ten paces before entering another room. There's tile everywhere, this must be the bathroom. I'm slammed down onto the fungus-inhabited, mildew rich shower floor, and the cold water is turned on. I try to get up but am restrained by half a dozen kids whose names I don't even know. Apparently, a deal had been made whereby if they did this favor for Silverstein and acted as his henchmen this one time, they would forever be spared his towel stealing antics.

The freezing water is streaming down my face and soaking my clothing. Shivering is literally the only thing I can do.

"Enough! Let me up."

I see D.A. hand one of the freshman a blade of some kind. My God. They're going to cut me up.

"D.A., aren't you overreacting a little bit?"

"Aren't you?"

It's then that I realize they're not cutting me so much as they are trying to shave me down.

Silverstein signals for the water to be shut off.
"Are you ready to act like a big boy, Matty?"
"Fuck you, fat ass."
The water is turned back on.
"Okay! Okay. I'm ready."
"We're going to let you up, Matt. But you have to swear to us to do two things."
"Anything."
"First, finish this shave job."
"Done."
"And next, get yourself together, man. So you can't date five women at once. Nobody can. Deal with it."
"You're the core of our group, Matt. We need you back."

And they're right. I need to shake this thing off. Don't get me wrong; no epiphany has been had. My situation seems just as grave now as it ever has. But at the same time, nobody got anywhere from pouting. If there is a solution out there, I won't find it in here, on the bathroom floor. And if not, well I had better find that out sooner than later so I can get on with it and hurl myself off of the Prominence Hotel roof.

***

It's only been three days since the intervention when the Mad Scientist calls me.

"The Journal of Behavioral Physiology and Neuroscience, Matthew!"

"Pardon me, sir?"

"Our publication made quite a splash. BP and N loves our work; they're rushing the process to get it into next week's issue."

"That's great, Professor."

"Great? It's a bloody miracle! I never thought we'd pull it together in time, but low and behold, we did it."

"Well you really deserve all of the credit, sir."

"Oh, nonsense. We're a team. And that's why when the controversy hits, I need you by my side as the face of our research."

Controversy? What controversy?

"You may not have been aware of the extent of it, Matthew, but our findings, especially the inferences made in the discussion section of the paper, are going to piss the hell out of a lot of people."

"The discussion section, right."

I've never read it. I was supposed to several dozen times over the preceding months but never had the incentive.

"I'm an old man, Matthew. I need your youth and imagination next to my age and wisdom when we appear on the talk shows."

"All do respect, sir, what the fuck are you talking about?"

"The talk shows! I never would have guessed it when we set out to begin this project, but apparently the predictive capabilities of analyses strikes a nerve when it comes to the general public. Apparently, there's some ethical debate about whether people would even *want* to know if they were on pace to develop Alzheimer's Disease at all! It's all going to make quite a splash in not only the scientific world but the *popular* scientific world as well! Who could have known?"

"And you want me to go on them with you? Why not take some of the more qualified research members? I won't know what to say."

"You've seen them, Matthew. You know that's not an option. I love the research team, but they'd be allergic to television cameras. You and I both know they're not the hippest, most presentable crowd."

"I guess it's you and me then, Prof."

"Alright! Now we're in business, Matthew. Come by the office tomorrow to talk more. Cheerio!"

Now, you're probably as confused as I am, but having just really read the paper for the first time, I'm starting to piece together the elements of this bizarre turn of events myself; maybe I can clarify some issues.

Apparently, a simple paper I wrote for the Mad Scientist's course inspired him to investigate a line of research which eventually far surpassed anything I could possibly comprehend. From what I can understand, the Mad Scientist and his team have developed a somewhat reliable method to manipulate neurons in the brain in such a way which allows them to reveal their future degenerative tendencies. To oversimplify, the scientists stimulate the neurons a certain way and count the density of those pre-Alzheimer's elements which can lead to the disease later in life. Thus, they have formulated an effective method of predicting advanced neuronal degeneration which is an area comprised of myriad diseases including but not limited to Alzheimer's. If you're still with me, you're a better neuro-student than I am because I, myself, just had to reread those sentences a couple of times to understand them—and I wrote it.

With the baby boomers approaching older age, and with the national life expectancy on the rise, millions more people than ever before are likely to be afflicted with these degenerative neuronal diseases which explains the public interest in a method which could predict the likelihood or pace of the degeneration. The ethical debate arises when you ask yourself whether or not you would actually want to know if you were likely to develop one of these diseases later in life. What if I let the Mad Scientist do his magic with a sample of my nervous system, and it turned out that on some divine schedule, I was slotted to develop Alzheimer's at the age of sixty five? In effect, assuming no unforeseen catastrophes, I would be living life with an expiration date of forty five more years at which point I would begin to lose all meaningful cognitive function. In my early twenties would I want to know this information? Would the knowledge make me live my life any differently? I've seen Maya's grandfather degenerate into senility, and it's nothing to look forward to. On the other hand, what if knowing your fate actually allowed you to alter it? If this test could serve as a wake up call for someone, if it could promote increasingly healthy lifestyles, then isn't it a boon for society? These are the issues which are apparently awaiting the Mad Scientist, myself, and an army of right-wing conservative talking heads on the local and national talk-show circuits.

A few weeks have passed now. At first, I roamed the campus in a daze—not quite believing that the Mad Scientist hadn't just lost his marbles. As it turned out, he hadn't. We got calls from countless radio and TV programs wanting us to stop by for an on-air chat. And not just local personalities but people who are nationally syndicated wanted to talk to us! It was quite a big deal, indeed. I let the Mad Scientist decide which shows we would do, and we did them. Before each appearance, I would be prepped by both producers of the show and Mad Scientist research assistants so that I could properly articulate remarks and charming retorts during the interviews. That was my role, after all—to be youthful and counterbalance the Mad Scientist's old age and overt madness. To be honest, I found the whole experience pretty easy to deal with. Everyone around me offered their advice as to how to avoid stiffening up in front of the camera, how to "just be yourself." I've never really understood that concept. Just being yourself is quite possibly the easiest task in the history of mankind; anyone can do it and everyone does. Even so, everyone seemed pleased with how well I performed. My parents said their phone doesn't stop ringing with complimentary calls. Seth said he was even able to hook up with a girl the other night strictly because she had heard of me.

I couldn't completely grasp the gravity of my fifteen minute's of quasi-fame's influence until I returned to campus the following week. See, I had cancelled my cell phone service out of fear to talk to any of my former women. I still felt a sickening lump in my throat crawl up every time I thought about Maya and that guy, and all the others would probably scream and throw things at me if they had the opportunity. Cowardly, yes. But also practical.

When I returned to campus, I realized that I had become one of those campus idols. People stared at me and whispered, "Is that him?" There were a dozens of posts about my appearances on the college message boards. One thread was titled, "insults and obscenities directed at Matthew Quibley." My favorite was a nice zinger a guest on one of the extremely conservative shows spewed my way: "Mr. Quibley obviously hates America and has no respect for moral responsibility or the laws it takes to protect a blasphemous nation from eternal damnation." Fuckin' Americans, always blowing their lid over nothing.

The problem with being a campus celebrity is that it makes it pretty hard to be a shadow. All of the big five poorly handled women in my life had either heard about my romantic misadventures or just assumed I was blowing them off after all this time without so much as a peep. A columnist for *The Herald* once wrote this column about how necessary it is for a temporary post-relationship lapse in communication and contact. He said that for any sort of amicable friendship to follow, time has to elapse in order for each party to forgive and get over the other. In my current situation, it's pretty hard to avoid contact with my five exes when I can't walk across the green without people on the other side noticing. Usually when I see one of them around, I avoid eye contact and pick up my pace. Only Gothic Gwyneth has had the chutzpah to accost me.

"Saw you on that morning show. You looked like crap."

I stop in my tracks and ponder my options. Keep walking? She'd likely follow me and cause a scene. I turn toward her and slowly raise my gaze from the ground toward her face. There is pain in it, and I feel my gut twist.

"Gwyneth, I'm sorry about—"

"Yeah. I got it." She softens a bit, but is still wary of me. "Don't let it all go to your head, Matt."

"Thanks. I'll remember that."

And with that, she was on her way.

***

Being a campus celebrity's not all bad, though. I try to look at the world in a pretty fair light, and it would be untrue to claim there were no perks at all. For one thing, a bouncer downtown let me in even though I had forgotten my ID at the dorm. It was a club downtown designated for jocks and hoodlums and I had never really been welcomed before. I am neither a jock nor a hoodlum, so what was I doing there? Well, a girl D.A. is interested in works behind the bar, and Silverstein told me it would be healthy to get out there and have a good time.

Looking around the place, it was pretty clear that the three of us didn't fit in. I began to scope the scene out, while D.A. and Silverstein trailed me arguing about which one of them the bouncer had laughed at on the way in. I had managed to take about three laps around the bar without recognizing anyone when I decided I had to ditch the guys. I love them to death, but sometimes they act as new people repellants when they're together. With a few well-executed moves and shimmies, I had managed to elude them. I was at the bar ordering a rum and coke when I feel a tap on the shoulder.

It's That Girl. She's tapping me on the shoulder, and I feel a spark in my body I haven't felt in weeks. I gaze into her with awe, and try to say hello. She's done down for a club, but I couldn't care less; she's still perfect to me.

"You're—"

She closes her eyes and swallows.

"You're that guy."

That Guy. Ha!

"Matt Quixley?"

"Quibley."

"Right, what did I say?"

She's drunk, but so damned cute.

"No, you got it right."

"I watched you on that show. That guy's show. You know the one I mean. He's been married like eight times and he wears suspenders."

"Yeah, what did you think?"

"You were very articulate."

"Thanks."

"Yeah, I don't remember what you said—I mean, not right now—but I remember being really impressed, and proud that you were representing my school. You know? You were so—"

Don't say it.

"You were just so *yourself* on camera."

Bah, I'll let it slide because it's That Girl.

A new song comes on. It's the typical repetitive dance beat with a retro sample interwoven into the song's chorus. I hate it. That Girl lights up like Silverstein when he's about to pounce on a freshman.

"I love this song," she exclaims.

"Me too."

"Let's dance."

And just like that, I was dancing with That Girl. We're bumping. We're grinding. A couple of other guys try to steal her away from me but she doesn't allow it. We dance. And we dance. And we dance. It gets hot in the heart of the club and we're both sweating, but it's a healthy sweat and she's not afraid to run her hands through my hair. When the lights come on at 2AM to banish us from the club, That Girl looks into my eyes and leans in. Normally I'd have kissed her, but not this night. Not this girl.

"I want you to come back with me, Max."

Fuck.

"I don't think I should."

"I want you to. Come on."

She leads takes my hand and leads me through the sea of people and out the club door. Within moments we're in one of her friend's cars. The designated driver is pissed to have to do it, but I try to smile at her. I don't want any trouble. In fact, the whole situation has me uneasy, but I don't have the wherewithal to resist any part of it.

The car pulls up to a house on Brooke Street, and we hop out. That Girl leads me onto her porch and searches her bag for her keys. After finding them, she drops them, picks them up, and drops them again. I bend down to pick it up for her and notice that the door is unlocked anyway. We enter to a dimly lit common room where a couple of her housemates have been smoking weed and watching a classic stoner movie I've never heard of in any other context. We say hello and she leads me into her room and latches the lock shut. Without hesitation she shoves me onto her bed and we begin an enthralling night of less than innocent sexual congress. Within an hour, we're both asleep, and I'm dreaming of being awake again.

The sun wakes me up before That Girl. It takes me two full seconds to remember where I am and what happened the night before. When I do remember, I can't help but smile. I look at That Girl and notice features about her I never have before. She has cuticles on the edges of her finger nails and a thin film of peach fuzz spanning her upper arms. From this close proximity, in a fully lit room, her imperfections are revealed to me. I find myself more intrigued than taken aback. Nobody's perfect. I know that. Getting a chance for a closer inspection, *this* is what I've been waiting for. I think.

I know I shouldn't, but I stroke her bare back gently, and she wakes up with a start. I see her piece together the necessary bits of information. Where is she? Who is touching her? Is she still drunk? Then a satisfied countenance falls upon her face as she has deemed the answers acceptable.

We get dressed, exchange numbers, and announce our intentions to get together later in the week. And we do just that. She has friends on the basketball team so we go to a game, and then the next night we see a movie, and then two nights after that we get drunk with her housemates and play trivia games.

At breakfast, Silverstein and D.A. question me over pancakes an entire week after that night at the club.

"So it's finally really happening for you?" D.A. asks.

I nod.

"I guess."

"You think it's the real deal?"

"I don't know."

"Well you better be sure."

Or else he'll put me away? Always the district attorney.

"Why's that, D.A.?"

"Because if you do this, if you keep this up, you're giving up on something you know is legit."

I look at him quizzically.

"Maya," Silverstein clarifies.

"You damned right, Maya. She's special, and you know it." Silverstein puts in his two cents. He's always been Maya's biggest fan.

"Yeah, well. I gave up on that a long time ago, didn't I?"

"It's not too late to get it back."

Now they're making me angry.

"What are you saying? Why would I want it back? I was suffocating, guys. Don't you know that by now? Why do you think I've engaged in all this madness?"

"And now you're not? This girl is really the one for you?" I know where Silverstein stands, but this is obviously D.A.'s show.

"I don't know. Maybe. You know how long I've pined after her."

"But you've never known her! You made her out to be this perfect image of a woman which she can't possibly live up to unless you, yourself, maintain the notion."

"We'll find out, won't we."

"What's so great about her, Matt? What is so fuckin' great exactly?"

"Well, she's hot for starters."
"Hotter than Maya?"
"No," Silverstein shouts.
"She's cool, and she's fun, and it's not always about the tangibles, okay?"
"Cooler, more fun than Maya?"
"What's with you guys? Why are you pushing agendas here? Why don't you just chill out and let me figure things out."

With that, I threw six bucks on the table and left the two idiots with each other at the breakfast joint.

***

I dated That Girl for the next three weeks, all the while putting up with Silverstein and D.A. pushing the Maya agenda. I can't help but feel the influence of their pushiness. Still, I try to put it out of my mind and give That Girl the chance she's earned in my mind, despite a general feeling of disappointment about the whole relationship.

Silverstein keeps saying that Maya wants to get together with me to talk things out. She even sent me a couple of emails and texts. I didn't think she was too serious, which is why I'm all the more surprised when she shows up at my door one Saturday morning. It is my door, but That Girl answers it. They greet each other awkwardly and Maya says that she had better go. That Girl insists that she is on her way out anyway. On her way out in her underwear? The tension sparks That Girl to move with super-human speed in getting dressed and out the door. Then Maya proceeds inside, sits down, and looks at me blankly. Blankly is not the right word. There is substance there, but it is too far beneath the surface for me to grasp.

"She's pretty."

I nod.

"How long have—?"

"A few weeks."

"How's it going?"

"Okay, I guess."

"She's really pretty."

"I know. So are you."

"I know."

There wasn't much anger between us, which is a phenomenon I wouldn't have expected.

"Are you seeing anyone?"

"Gilbert was giving me a hard time about moping so I went on this sort-of date with this guy from my Chem class."

"The one who's been asking you out all semester?"

She nods.

"It didn't go very well. There was only the one time."

"Did you know I was messing around with other girls?"

"Yeah. I thought so, and your boys confirmed it when I pressured them enough."

Sons of bitches.

"Is that why you 'sort of hooked up' with that guy?"

"Maybe it played a role. It definitely made it easier to justify, I guess."

"How did you know about it before they told you?"

"You're not the best at deception, Matt. How many were there, four?"

I nod.

"You had four distinct moods and areas of excuses that you'd use when you went to see them."

"Areas of excuses?"

"Yeah, you know. Work, guy time, exercise, and stress. You didn't even realize, did you? You used each of them at distinctive times and I pretty much knew which one you were going to."

"Are you bullshitting me?"

She shakes her head.

"You should have a detective show on TV or something."

"No, I shouldn't. That's what I'm saying. If you want to be one of those guys, the ones who do these sorts of things, you need a better poker face, Matt."

For five seconds we look at each other from six feet apart and let our emotions silently fill the space between us. I miss Maya. I do, and I don't know what to do about it.

"You're full of shit, you know?"

"Yeah, but how do you mean?"

"Silverstein explained to me your Mormon theorizing."

"It wasn't Mormon. It was masculine."

"That's the part that's bullshit."

She's using obscenities but it's casual usage. At no point do I feel like she's really displeased with me. We're just having a discussion—which is weird considering the circumstances.

"You think men are the only ones with needs?"

"No. I just think they're different needs than women have."

"Yeah, you're right, but not in the way you think."

"You know how I think, Maya?"

"Yes. Men are programmed to spread their seed. Evolutionarily the ones who do have a better chance of procreating and sending their genetic codes into future generations. Right? More than one girl makes evolutionary sense, right? Cheating, makes evolutionary sense for a man, right?"

"Yeah. More or less."

She was always smarter than me, and I wonder where she's going with this.

"And a woman is inclined to be prude because if she gets pregnant, it's a nine month or life-long investment. She had better wait 'til she finds that one worthwhile guy and hold onto him and make sure she keeps him happy. Right?"

"Sure."

"No. It's wrong. Evolutionarily, it's wrong. I'd have thought that since you had given this topic so much thought you'd have come up with the more logical answer by now."

"You give me too much credit."

"Always have."

"So enlighten me, babe."

"Well, you're partly right in that women are more selective about who they settle down with and are more prone to try to hold onto that guy because he is best suited for the desired patriarchal role.

Also, maybe we tend to select guys who are dependable and reliable and overall good providers. But is that who women tend to cheat with?"

"No. They cheat with jocks and meatheads."

"Right. And you don't see that as evolutionarily predisposed?"

I don't.

"How is it?"

"Women want that reliable, responsible guy to be there to provide for and raise their children, right? But they don't want those kids to be the biological children of the good guys. They want the sperm of the bad guys, the 'jocks and meatheads,' and they want the good guys to raise them."

"Holy hell. That's every good guy's worst nightmare."

"I know. But it makes sense doesn't it?"

"Yes. I can't believe I never thought about it like that. Women are predisposed to fuck the football team and marry the tech house. The football team gives them the athletic genes and the tech house provides food and shelter after they invent the personal computer. No shit. I'm stunned."

"Well anyway, no one's perfect, right? Not you, and not me."

She stands up and hugs me.

"Do you think this girl—"

"That Girl."

"What?"

"Nothing. Sorry for interrupting. Go on."

"Do you think you'll overcome evolution being with her?"

"I don't know."

"Well, I hope you do."

"Thanks, Maya."

"I'll see you around."

And with that, she walks out of my room. In an instant, without warning, Maya has become the new That Girl and That Girl has become the new Maya. Fuck.

For the next two weeks, every internal effort to enjoy myself with That Girl disintegrates. I start noticing things about her which are entirely unattractive in nature. For starters, she's a bit of a ditz and may have a drinking problem. Our conversations just aren't there. We talk, but nothing ever gets said. The other day she asked me what I was thinking; I couldn't tell her that I was thinking of how nice it was to be silent. Also, I think she gave me a rash.

I wish I didn't have to tell you this. I wish it were different, that I could say that That Girl and I had a fairy tale ending—that we overcame life's urges and were truly happy. But usually life doesn't work out exactly the way you hope it does.

Eventually, I knew I had to proceed with the inevitable, and I broke up with That Girl. We were at this artsy tea shop on Thayer Street, the kind of place where they play independent chill music and have student art on the walls. I don't think she was too upset when I did the deed. She sort of just nodded and finished her tea with me. She didn't ask why; we both knew it was just the simple fact that in the end we didn't stimulate each other all that much. As a wise old college student, it has become clear to me that some people click, and some don't. In the beginning of relationships, it's much easier to convince yourself that you click with someone because there are that many more question marks to keep you stimulated. After a while though, you just have to face the facts. And it was that time for That Girl and me.

You may be wondering whether I immediately called Maya, shallow and fickle as I am. Well I didn't. I want to, but I have to draw the line somewhere. Nobody's perfect, but she deserves better than what I've been able to give her in the past. I know that now.

Maybe my fate is to be unsatisfied and alone. I've still got Silverstein to keep me laughing, so that's something.

With the subject of girls completely vanquished from my mind, about 85% of my cerebral resources have been freed up. What have I used this newfound brainpower to do? Nothing really exciting. I've really delved into my school work, more than I would have otherwise. I used to think that physics was an all or none phenomenon with regard to understanding it. It turns out that I was wrong. Having a predisposition for understanding the material, being able to speak the language of science, is a start and is usually sufficient to get by, but it just so happens that when I really apply myself and devote some time and energy to studying, windows open all throughout my mind. I'm beginning to see the world more clearly.

The second endeavor taking up most of my time, besides keeping an eye on the fellas, is working out. They say endorphins are released when you exercise, and they suppress pain and enable certain highs. Well, I don't know about all that, but I'll tell you that it feels good to use my body again. I once learned about a psychologist—I can't remember his name—but he thought there were half a dozen different types of intelligence (e.g. mathematical, spatial, verbal, etc). The one which most psych students find hardest to believe exists is called kinesthetic intelligence. Basically, it entails being physically able. In a sense, professional athletes are brilliant in kinesthetic intelligence. Just like with all the other kinds of smarts, everyone is born with a certain level of natural ability. But one's performance is not solely derived from this birthright unless he allows himself to be complacent. If he works at it, lifts weights, and exercises his heart and body, he will reach levels of kinesthetic intelligence otherwise out of his original ability range. I don't know why I'm telling you about this, but the point is that when I started I could hardly do a pull-up and now I can do a dozen. If I'm ever grasping for my life at the edge of a cliff, I'll be able to pull myself up easy—and besides, I look better naked this way. I kid, but the truth is that since I'm transferring much of my sexual energy toward exercise, I'm much less concerned with the topic these days.

I settle into a routine which lasts a couple of months before I have to take a respite due to illness. There's been an outbreak on campus; some twenty-four hour bug is going around, giving everyone flu-like symptoms.

I'm in bed watching a soap opera entirely in Spanish when Silverstein walks into the room with a guest. It's Maya. She's got soup.

"Silverstein told me you weren't feeling so great. Wanna let the EMT have a look?"

"I'll let you know if I need someone to stabilize my neck, thanks."

"Hey! I do more than that."

"I know."

"I clean up a lot of vomit, too."

She hands me the soup and I take it and thank her. Silverstein excuses himself, a surprising show of consideration for him.

"You look like hell. Will you let me take care of you?"

"I don't want to make you sick."

"I had it last week. I'll be fine."

She lies down in bed next to me and into the Maya crevice which has been vacant for quite some time.

"I miss this. I miss you. I mean, I'm fine, but I would be better if we were together I think."

"I think you deserve better than me, Maya."

"I know, but *you* deserve me, and *I* deserve to be happy, so where does that leave us?"

"It won't work."

"Why not? We're not animals," she says. "We can do it. Just be *man* enough."

"In two months, I'm going to California for grad school."

"I'll come with you. Or I won't. We'll worry about it in two months."

I would be lying if I said I hadn't thought about what it would be like to be back with Maya. To start fresh. No. Not to start fresh, but to start over as a wiser person.

"Would you cheat on me again, Matt?"

"No."

"But you'd want to."

"Probably, yeah. But you'd be the same way."

"Yeah."

Thirty seconds of silence with no movement. We're too content. Will it last? Certainly not. I'll get restless, and she'll demand more of me than I can happily give. If our satisfaction lasts the two remaining months of the school year, it will be completely worth it, though.

"So?"

I look into her eyes gazing up upon me from the Maya crevice. I kiss her as if it were for the first time. Please let this last. I am asking, no, pleading for mercy. Let this last. Please let it last.

I know it won't though. Such is life as the Insatiable Man.

Acknowledgements

This novella could not have been written and published if it weren't for the support of my friends and family.

I first need to thank the lovely and talented Michaela Labriole, without whom this novella would never been finished. Her support of and belief in my endeavors never ceases to inspire me.

I would also like to thank David Reidy and Christopher Elias for their creative insights.

Justin Iorio was kind enough to contribute the cover art for this work.

Lastly, I need to thank Evan Brown for his editorial guidance during the writing process of *Insatiable*.

978-0-595-43219-6
0-595-43219-0

Printed in the United States
70929LV00002B/4-21